THE STRAW

TRAP

A Victorian Romance

by

Janet Hutcheon

PROLOGUE

It was October 1851 and the Luton petty sessions courtroom smelled of wet wool and the stale sweat of many bodies. Rebecca crept to the back of the crowded room and perched on a bench behind a large woman she did not recognise whose fingers were busy with bonnet plait. The result of the woman's industry trailed over her lap and lay in a loop on the worn wooden floor. Rebecca craned around her but could not see her mother or the table where the magistrates sat. She had seen the mayor before but the other men who were to judge her mother were unknown to her.

Somewhere, down at the front, sat Mr Roberts, the plait dealer, the accuser, the enemy. There was whispering and a few heads turned to look at Rebecca in her patched and faded dress as she slid into her seat. Her heart beat fast and she was overcome with shame. Tucking her worn and mud- stained boots under the bench, she flattened the torn front of her pinafore. What would the family do if they sent her mother to prison?

The woman in front reached across to take another split of straw from the bundle held under her arm. She drew it across her mouth to moisten it then worked the end into her work and continued to plait as she listened. Rebecca knew the feel of that straw, the pattern of movements in her own fingers. Her own lips were sore and her fingers rough from the same automatic toil repeated hour after hour, day after day, for almost as long as she could remember.

Ever since her father died, the family had subsisted only on what they could earn from the plaiting. Fortunately her mother was skilled and swift, having learned it as a young girl, as did all the children in Bedfordshire and beyond. Even boys were put to the learning of it as toddlers, as most expected to become agricultural workers from the age of fourteen. Wages for their fathers were low and often intermittent, especially in the winter when everyone turned to plaiting straw to bring in a few extra pence per week.

Rebecca lived in Lilley, a village a good way on the road from Luton to Offley. Beyond that was Hitchin but Rebecca had never been there. Her mother went to Luton to the plait market but Rebecca had never been there either so everyone in the room was unknown to her. Nevertheless, there was not a woman anywhere in the neighbourhood who didn't spend all her waking hours plaiting. They walked in the street chatting, their fingers unceasing. They walked in the fields plaiting. Homes were often neglected, for the plaiting was important; it was often all a family had to stave off starvation.

'State your case, Mr Roberts.' The mayor's voice was imperious. There was a rustling and a murmuring but then Mr Roberts' voice rose above the assembly.

'I left three score of plait with Jane Chapman while I visited the inn on private business. I buy 'er plait on a Monday but when I returned an hour later, she weren't there. Only the child were there an' she said 'er mother 'ad gone to the plait market to sell 'er scores and buy new straw.'

4

'And your own plait?'

'Gone, Sir. I took the trouble to look aroun' the room but it was gone.'

'So it was your opinion that the accused had taken your plait to sell as her own?'

'Indeed it were, Sir.'

'What made you so sure of that?'

'Poverty, Sir, and no man in the 'ouse. Nuthin' but an old stove, some old sticks, chairs and stuff as far as I could see.'

'What did you do?'

'I went along to the market to catch 'er. I found 'er standin' in line with all the women waitin' to sell and when I got 'er by the arm and claimed my three score, she cried she was falsely accused. It was then I called the constable, Sir.'

There was no sound in the room except for the breathing and coughing of the listening crowd. Rebecca recalled the big man with his heavy brows and big hands, stamping around their small cottage, wrenching

5

her arm and pushing his face close as he questioned her. She had told him what her mother had told her to say, fearfully spluttering out the words.

'Is the girl here?' asked the magistrate, and Rebecca's heart leapt with alarm. She crouched low in her seat and tucked in her head.

Someone was speaking. 'The girl is not here so we cannot call her.' There was a pause and then she heard, 'Oh, very well. Is there anyone else to speak for Jane Chapman? No? Then let us hear what she has to say for herself.'

Her mother's voice was heavy with bitterness. 'I was not meaning to steal the plait. I was takin' it to meet Mr Roberts on my way to the market. I wanted a better price than he give me for my own plait. I didn't want to miss the best offers.'

'Why did you not take the plait to the inn to meet him?'

'Because it was out of my way and I was worrying about the time.'

'And what time of day was it?'

'I don' know, Sir. Some time in the afternoon.'

Roberts spoke up. 'It was just after two. I know because…'

'And the market shuts at five? Six? Plenty of time to sell your own plait. What have you to say, Mrs Chapman?'

Desperation sounded in her mother's voice. 'But the prices are too low later on.'

There was a murmur of voices as the men on the bench discussed the matter. Then the mayor asked, 'Where is your husband, Mrs Chapman?'

'He were killed two year ago, up on Ward's farm.'

'And you have no other income but the plaiting?'

'No, Sir.'

'So it is true that extra plait to sell would add to your income. Whereas I am not of the opinion that poverty always turns honest folk into thieves, I am inclined to find for Mr Roberts. However, you did not sell the plait.

I therefore fine you two pounds with a fortnight to pay. Case dismissed.'

There was a stirring and shifting in seats and the coughing of tight lungs. All eyes turned on Jane Chapman as she walked to the door at the back of the room. Rebecca was blind to the weathered faces of the men, the pale bonneted women, their smirks and frowns. She saw only her mother walking stiffly between them in her shabby grey dress. Her head was held high and her mouth was a straight line. As she drew level, Rebecca slipped off the bench, took her mother's hand and walked with her out of the room.

Part One

Chapter 1

Ahead lay the long road out of the town towards Offley
and Hitchin beyond. With her head held high, Jane
strode on. It was a good five miles to the turn off to
Lilley, through the village and on to their cottage. The
day was cold and she drew her shawl tightly around her
shoulders, her face set in a firm expression, giving no
hint of the anger inside. She had thrown off her
daughter's hand, not realising that Rebecca was
struggling to keep up. On hearing the plaintive 'Ma,' she
paused, still too choked with anger to speak, while
Rebecca ran to catch up.

Two pounds, for her a tremendous amount of money,
had to be found somehow and all because the plait
dealer was a lying, cheating, vengeful man intent on
forcing his will on her. For this they had been forced to
walk to Luton and now had the long trek home, past the
cobblers and bookmakers, the draper's shop and the

milliner's, past the houses, and out of town to the country road with Rebecca running behind.

How could they earn the extra money in two weeks? Jane slowed slightly to save her breath and turned to make sure that Rebecca was behind her. The girl would help, but it was going to be hard for her, losing sleep and sitting for long hours of the day and night when her young fingers were still soft. Dare they spend tuppence on a lift with a carrier to save the child's legs? No, now they could not afford even this small expense.

Rebecca had stopped to pick a handful of blackberries from the hedgerow to quieten her hunger.

'Hurry, Beccy,' Jane called. 'We've no time to lose.'

Rebecca ran forward. 'Maybe he won't call no more, Ma.'

'I would love to have nothing more to do with him but he won't be so easy to refuse,' Jane replied through gritted teeth. 'But who else will take our scores?'

A score was the standard twenty yards of plaited straw for sewing into hats and bonnets. Silas Roberts was the only dealer who called round all the cottages in Lilley and Jane knew he offered prices per score less than those she would get from the plait market. It saved good plaiting time to sell to him, and it saved the walk, especially if the weather was bad. She would prefer not to sell to Roberts, but there was no other option but the long walk to Luton and back every Monday. The dealer's words in the courtroom had stung her. When Dan had been alive there was some hope of avoiding the slow slide into poverty. There was more in their cottage than the 'sticks and stuff' Roberts had described, but not much more. Anything she could sell had already gone and only the necessary basics remained. Dan had brought in a weekly wage from his work on the farm. He had been a good worker, loyal and conscientious, and Arthur Ward had valued him. Now, of course, there was no weekly wage, no money at all except what Jane and Rebecca could earn by the plaiting.

It was the same all over the county and had been for years. The money Dan earned from his farm work was hardly enough keep a growing family so, like every

11

other woman, Jane had found the plaiting a good way to bring in a few extra shillings.

A horse and cart came along behind them and they stepped into the side of the lane to let it pass. It was not the carter but Jethro Ward, Mr Ward's eldest. Instead of going by, he drew to a halt beside them.

'I'm going your way, Jane Chapman. I'll offer you a lift, you and the girl.' He smiled down at Rebecca in a friendly way.

'I can manage, Jethro.' Her mother's shut-in face avoided his eyes.

'You going to make that little mite walk another three mile?' He leaned forward and waited.

Jane's face softened as she turned to him. Jethro was a year older but she had known him on and off all her life, especially at the annual harvest suppers his father gave for his men, when she had even danced a jig with him. Dan had given her reports of Arthur Ward as a decent employer and a good family man. His son had grown into a fine young man with brown curly hair and steady brown eyes. Years of farm work had given him strong shoulders, as were the hands that held the reins.

'Get up, Rebecca, and thank you, Jethro,' Jane said after a moment's thought.

They jolted along the lanes, the horse's tail swishing the flies away and the cart wheels rumbling over the stony ground. The extra height allowed them to see over the hedges, to the fields where the golden corn had been harvested and the foliage of the beets were beginning to curl in the late autumn sun. Jane glanced at Jethro beside her. The cloth of his working trousers was stretched tightly over his thighs and reminded her of Dan. She felt a jolt in her heart and a stirring of the old sorrow deep inside. She gave a sigh; she had been almost two years without him. Jethro's handsome face was relaxed and pleasant. 'How is your father?' she asked to take her mind off the physicality that had suddenly disturbed her.

'He's fine. Still mighty sorry about Dan. We miss him, apart from the loss of him doubling my duties.'

She nodded her agreement. 'Mine too.'

'I imagine so. Father'd like to help, I know.'

13

Jane lifted her chin and looked ahead. 'We'll manage,' she said as they drove through the village at last.

His father's farm was beyond the village on the track to Ward's Wood, passing their own cottage where he stopped. As Jane alighted and reached to help Rebecca down they shared a glance, then, haltingly as if slightly discomfited, he said, 'Are you still selling to Roberts after this?'

'Don't concern yourself over me, Jethro.'

'I'll likely be going to Luton next Monday. I can give you a lift, if you like.'

'That's very kind, Jethro, but I'll not be beholden to you.'

He looked across at the firm mouth, frowned briefly and nodded, then flicked the reins and went on his way, leaving the two to trudge down the muddy path to their door.

Like so many others, the cottage had two rooms, one up and on12 down, and was stone built with a thatched roof which overhung the front, forming a small porch. In his spare time Dan had filled in the cracks of the stonework and fixed the wooden window frames to keep out the draughts. Recently, however, the winter storms had damaged the thatch and allowed the rain to drip through into the upstairs room. However, there were other cottages nearby in worse condition than theirs, randomly built along the lane, each with a growing family of noisy children and less concern for the mud and mess that collected around them.

Now, as they walked into the one room where they had lived so happily, Jane's thoughts were still coloured by the memory of her loss. Looking round the room, now so devoid of all that had been comforting and hopeful, she steeled herself against the onslaught of those sorrowful feelings. The rough whitewashed stone walls were losing their brightness and the planks of the floor were littered with cut straw she had not had time to sweep up. On the far wall was the chimney alcove with its now almost dead fire in the grate and a full ashcan beneath. A cooking pot hung from the metal bracket.

Dan had put up two shelves to the left of the fire with hooks fixed under the lower shelf intended for their pots and utensils, and from the beams over their heads, had strung a line from which there now hung the girls' aprons, chemises and underskirts and Stevie's shirts she had washed the day before.

There was food to be ready for Nancy and Stevie when they came home from the plait school. They went every day except Sunday. Usually Rebecca fetched them home and took them back for the afternoon session. Bread, a stub of cheese and cold tatties would have to do for today.

The room was chilled and dark except where a shaft of the midday sun shone through the small window on to the wooden table in the middle of the room. There was one decent backed chair which had been for Dan, two other wooden chairs and two stools, one of which held a washing bowl and a kettle for heating water, fetched from the well. A collection of mugs and plates and a dish or two stood on the upper of the two shelves. In the darkest corner was a day bed with one blanket on a straw mattress and a cushion for Stevie's head that Jane had sewn and stuffed with rags. There had once been a picture or two, a vase, a cloth rug and some glasses but these were long gone, sold a couple of years before when coping alone with three hungry children had tested Jane's strength to the utmost.

They had such plans in the happy days, such plans for advancement, but these days Jane tried not to think of that time or of Dan, for the sense of loss overwhelmed her. He had wanted more than farm work and, unlike the men around them, dared to be ambitious. The only work in the villages was agricultural and although Arthur Ward had been a good boss there were few opportunities for promotion in such a small concern. At fourteen years old Dan had been put to the ploughing and over the years had learned all the other skills the farm had to offer. He was quick and reliable, good with the cattle and sheep, and Mr Ward paid him well.

Jane remembered one of the days he came home late and tired and once again had voiced his dissatisfaction. 'Ward says the wheat and the barley will fetch him less

17

this year. That means wages will be lower, eight shillings this week instead of twelve, I shouldn't wonder. Thank God for the plaiting, Jane. Can you manage more hours, do you think?'

Jane had looked over at the man she loved, now weary of the constant toil. Already his hair was grey at the temples yet still he was a young man.

'I can try. Nancy is coming on nicely with the Brilliant style of plait, and will manage a couple of shillings, and Rebecca, maybe three more. Will Ward have any more hours he can give you?'

'It's tough for him too. I know for a fact he's going to lay off a couple of the men in the next week or so.'

'As long as he keeps you on.'

'I've half a mind to try my hand elsewhere, brewing or brick making, even stonework. There's work to be had in Luton, I know.'

'But we'd have to give up the cottage, and where would we go? You'd have to learn new skills and that means low wages.'

'It's not seasonal, though. We planned it, remember. I was going to try the hat factories.'

'But there would be more travelling, higher prices and bosses who are cutthroat and greedy.'

'I'll not like leaving Arthur Ward in the lurch, I must say.'

Jane ran her hand over the small bulge fast growing under her pinafore. This was not the time to tell him she was pregnant.

Jane sat slumped before the dying embers of their small fire. Could they do it between them, her and Rebecca? Her heart sank at the prospect of the long days ahead. With a sigh, she put her hands over her face but then removed them for Rebecca was looking at her anxiously. She must hide her despair from the children, especially her eldest daughter who felt everything so keenly. And Stevie was a worry too.

When Stevie was born Dan was stuck. They dare not take the risk of moving. Of course he was pleased to have a son but the little mite was a troublesome infant.

19

Since then he had grown into a sickly child, sweet-natured but often ill.

Just as Rebecca was leaving to fetch the little 'uns from the school, their neighbour Jessie called out from the path. 'Cooee, Jane, are you there?'

Jessie and her unruly family lived in the next cottage along the lane, in the shade of the trees. Despite its obvious dilapidation, it housed Jessie and her seven children and a lodger as well. Jane had decided a long time ago that Jessie was a slattern, a large woman with a loud voice and a complaining nature, and she tried to have as little contact as possible. She groaned inwardly as she met Jessie at the door.

'You feelin' neighbourly today, Jane? Could your Becca fetch my two youngest from the plait school this midday? I ain't got the time and as she's goin' for your Nancy and Stevie, p'raps she could bring my two as well.'

Jane paused and eyed the woman's filthy clothes and tried not to wrinkle her nose at the smell that assailed her. 'I was planning on getting Nancy to start that duty,

Jess. Rebecca and I will be plaiting all the hours God sends from now on. Couldn't your Flo fetch your two?'

'I knows about your trouble. That Roberts is a right bastard. Flo ain't that well at the moment and Maisie downright refuses, so I'm stuck. I'll pay Rebecca twopence a week if she would do it reg'lar, like.'

Jane looked over at Rebecca, standing all ears close by. Jessie had two teenage sons working on local farms, a thirteen-year-old earning a little scaring birds and the two daughters plaiting at home with Jessie. The lodger must pay something for a place to sleep though how they all managed in one upstairs room was a mystery. There was surely enough money coming in for Jessie to afford tuppence a week on top of the fourpence she paid the plait mistress at the school. However, an extra couple of pence a week was not an offer Jane could refuse.

'All right,' she said, 'Rebecca can do it today but then Nancy must take over. She's coming up to seven but can manage Stevie, and your two.'

When Jessie had gone Rebecca said, 'Aw, Ma, do I have to?'

'Only today, Beccy. I want you here plaiting alongside me. We've got to make the scores or I can't pay the fine.'

'Nancy won't like it. That little Joey is a devil, always making trouble, and he smells.'

'Never mind that. Tuppence is tuppence. Now go or you'll be late.'

When Rebecca had gone, Jane mentally totted up the money she would have to spend out of her small reserves. She knew there was rent to pay at a shilling a week, flour, soap, sugar and tea to buy. Then there were bundles of straw at sixpence a pound for them to plait and money for the plait school for the little 'uns. How could they afford all these necessities and pay the fine as well? There was no way but the plaiting. They would have to do more, into the night if necessary.

Already the evenings had begun drawing in and soon they would need candles. Candles and fuel were an added expense. Rebecca earned three shillings a week for her work but she was getting quicker. Jane earned more because she could do the more complicated English Pearl and Brilliant designs but it was still not enough and now Roberts wouldn't call at the house any more. Perhaps she had been rash to refuse Jethro's offer of a lift. The long walk every Monday to the plait market and back would use up a serious amount of plaiting time. She regretted speaking so harshly to Beccy. She was a good girl, too aware at her young age of the stress and worry of their situation.

In readiness for the children's lunch, she put the bowl of cold potatoes and the bread on the table and cut the cheese into three small pieces. The remaining crust and rind was her own lunch and she chewed as she worked, then heard another knock at the door. It was Silvie, her friend from the village. As soon as she opened up, Silvie almost fell into the room.

'Jane, I had to come. I've just heard. It's all over the village. What are you going to do?'

Jane gave a heavy sigh. 'There's nothing I can do except work even harder. Beccy will help me but it will be tough.'

'You know I would help you if I could but two pounds?   Silvie shook her head sadly.

'No Silvie, I wouldn't ask you. This is our problem.'

'What I can't understand is why that man is picking on you.'

'It's because I won't do exactly what he wants.'

'He's just like all the rest of the dealers. I don't trust any of them. You hear such tales.'

'Oh, you don't know the half of it, Silvie. Silas Roberts and I go back a long way, or at least since I was sixteen.'

'But you weren't living here then.'

'No, I was in Herts with my parents. Sixteen and stupid. Look, I don't want to talk about how naive I was.'

'Well, we all do stupid things when we are young.'

'I'll just say that he thinks he has a claim on me and wants to bring me down. When I can't get any lower, then I'll turn to him – that's what he thinks.'

'That's terrible, but everyone will do their best to help.'

Jane leaned closer to her friend. 'No Silvie, please don't tell anyone. I can't explain any more. You won't tell anyone, will you?'

At that moment, the sound of children's voices was heard on the path outside. Silvie picked up her shawl and made for the door. 'Alright, if that's what you want, but I'd better go or my Suzy won't get any dinner.'

Rebecca hurried in, pulling Stevie behind her, his dull blonde hair flopping over his face, his short legs with knees like knots in a piece of string stumbling behind.

Jane hurried them to the table. 'What kept you all? Hurry now and eat.'

'Ma, it was that Joey, he kept going off and I had to chase after him.'

Stevie sat on a stool, chewing his bread. 'He threw
a stone at me, Ma. He's a big boy. I don't like him.'

'Well, if he does that again, I'll talk to his mother.'
Nancy, you'll have to come home on your own with
Stevie, and Joey and Dody too from now on. I need
Rebecca with me all day now.'

'Oh Ma, I don't want to do it. Those two are dirty
and smelly.'

'Hush Nancy, you are old enough to look after Stevie
and the other two. You'll get twopence a week for
bringing them both home at the end of the day. Not
lunch time. There's no need for that.' She would have a
word with Jessie and amend their arrangement.

Stevie swallowed and said, 'I like Dody. She's four
like me.'

Nancy pointed a finger at him and put on a severe
face. 'You'll have to do what I say now because I'm in
charge.'

Jane asked, 'What did you do this morning, Stevie?'

'We sang a song and I picked the straws.'

'Did you do any letters?'

'No, we just plaited. Nancy showed me plain plait.'

'Can you do it?'

'A bit.'

'He can't, Ma. He did some rolling, though. I did two yards of plain. Mrs James is going to show me the Pearl next week and let me use the splitting tool. She says I've got a gift for it.'

'Two yards is good, Nancy. Now, eat up or you'll be late back.'

Stevie got down gingerly from the stool and stood before her with his head on one side. 'Do I 'ave to, Ma? I got a sore shoulder.'

Jane tutted but pulled him closer to her. 'Let me see.' She pulled down the neck of his shirt to the swollen red lump under his collar bone. 'Gracious, what is this? Nancy did you see this happen?'

'It was the stone. Joey threw it and when it hit Stevie he laughed. Stevie didn't cry but I could see it hurt him,' the girl said.

Jane was aghast. She'd had in mind a small pebble but this must have been more the size of a brick. She looked wide-eyed at them both. 'I'm not having this. Stevie you must go to school now and I'll rub some lard on it when you come home. Ask Mrs James to let you off the work this afternoon. Nancy, if Joey throws any more stones, tell him he'll be in big trouble.'

'I don't think it will make any difference, Ma,' Nancy said.

Jane frowned as she stood. 'It will when I've had a word with his mother. Now, off you go.'

CHAPTER 2

Jane worried about her son. His had not been an easy birth and he was prone to numerous colds and coughs throughout the year. She tried to build up his strength by feeding him as well as she could, hoping he would become as strong and vigorous as his sisters. But he had gone downhill when his father died and had never quite got over his loss.

After instructing Rebecca to sit close to the window where the light was best and to plait without stopping until she returned, Jane grabbed her shawl and made for the cottage down the lane where Jessie lived. She knew enough about the woman to know she was a careless mother, happy to sit plaiting the whole day and let the care of the children go hang. In the same two rooms there were numerous children and Jane was not convinced they all had the same father. Jessie's husband had lived with them for a while but now he was long gone and a lodger had arrived. Jessie had three older

29

sons, Doug, Wally and Davy and two younger girls, Maisie and Flo, and the two youngest, Joey and Dody. Jane suspected that these last two were sired by the lodger. Counting the lodger and Jessie, that made nine bodies, but such overcrowding was not unusual in this village.

Their cottage sat in the shade of a clump of trees and was dark and damp. Some attempt to revive the neglected garden had once been attempted by the lodger but now she was sure he turned up only to sleep and perhaps eat. Too close to the door was a heap of garbage and waste to which was added the night soil of nine people which might have manured the garden but now oozed a stink that wrinkled Jane's nose as she approached.

'Jessie, are you there?' Jane called. There was a pause but then the badly fitting door swung creakily open and Jessie stood, holding closed the neck of her blouse with one hand.

'What is it?' the woman said, seeming mightily discomfited by Jane's appearance. Through the open doorway Jane could see the shadow of a man in the interior. As usual the floor was littered with straw cutoffs, left from their labours for days on end. She supposed that like many other women Jessie thought this a flattering testament to her unceasing industry.

'Your Joey has been throwing stones. My Stevie has a bruise the size of a hen's egg on his back. You can forget our arrangement if he can't behave. I'll not have my brood blinded or hurt by one of yours.'

Jessie gave a short laugh. 'Surely you're making a lot of a little. They're boys. What do you expect? It's what boys do.'

'Don't include my Stevie in this. He doesn't throw stones at people.'

Jessie was holding the open door with one hand and now she made a dismissive gesture with the other, allowing her blouse to fall open around her substantial shoulders. She tutted as she gathered the torn ends together again and looked stonily at Jane.

Jane folded her arms, determined to say her piece. 'Your Joey is a mite too unruly for my Nancy to cope with. She can bring them home at the end of the day but not at lunchtime, no.'

Jessie frowned. 'That ain't what we agreed. That's five times less a week. Can't pay twopence a week for five times less. Can't your Nancy give Joey a thick ear if he gets out of hand? It's what I do.'

'And have him punch her back? He's almost as big as she is.'

'Yes, well, my kids aren't feeble weaklings,' Jessie said, implying that Jane's were. 'Why don't Rebecca take them?'

'The same reason you don't get Maisie or Flo to fetch your two,' Jane said smartly.

'Ah, plaitin' will take up all your time now, I fancy. He's a mighty demandin' man, that Roberts. When you goin' to learn how to manage 'im, like I do.'

'I don't intend to learn to manage him,' Jane replied.

'Then more fool you, Jane. He's easy to satisfy.'

Jane half turned and looked out over the mess around the cottage. 'Satisfy him? That I shall never do.'

'Then I wish you luck. You surely got to learn which side your bread's buttered with no man around these days.'

The tack the whole conversation had taken was anathema to Jane. She changed the subject. 'Look, can't you give your two some food in their pockets for the lunchtime break? They could eat it in the street like several others do as they play.

'Awright, but I give you one penny and a half for that.'

Jane guessed that tuppence would have made only the smallest dent in Jessie's income but she'd had enough of this conversation so she agreed, and made her way home.

As Jane hurried back home, her head seethed with irritation. She wasn't sure she had impressed Jessie with the seriousness of her complaint. Throwing stones could take out an eye – she had heard of such things. Nor was she sure she had made her concern for her children clear enough. It wasn't beyond Joey's power to do worse if Jessie did nothing to curb his wild behaviour.

She found Rebecca hard at work, a tail of plait she had finished looped on her lap. Drawing up a chair, Jane sat beside her and started work, the first of her day. Her mind continued to brood on Stevie. Had circumstances been different she might have kept him at home for another year for he was young for his age. Some children were sent even as infants, mostly to leave their mothers a clear day for plaiting. At home she might have taught him to read but now all that was impossible. She also worried that she had told Silvie too much about Roberts and sent her away speculating on what shameful thing Jane had done. She could tell Silvie was curious, but she was a good friend and had been a tower of strength when Dan died, and could surely be relied upon to keep a confidence.

As four o'clock approached she made up her mind to meet the children out of the school, watch how they walked together and check there was no more stone throwing.

'Have a little break, Beccy. I just want to make sure all is well with Nancy. I may have a word with Mrs James if I get the chance but I won't be long.'

As it happened, Jane arrived outside the school before the children were released. Mrs James was a widow and used her downstairs room for instructing the children. Her only income, Jane supposed, were the multiple tuppences she collected from the parents of her pupils.

The walls of the cottage had once been white but were now stained and weathered. On the other side of the door, she could hear the voices of children of all ages, from three to seven, singing a plait song.

Over one and under two.

Pull it tight and that will do.

She pushed open the door and a gust of stale air hit her. About thirty children were crowded together in the small room, with little space to move their elbows. Some of the youngest crawled on the straw-littered floor in front of the schoolmistress. The rest were on benches and stools, each with a length of their handiwork in their fingers. They started learning to plait at five years and by six were expected to be competent enough to earn a few pence a week.

Seeing her in the doorway, Nancy stood up and, climbing over the other children, picked up Stevie and made for the door. The mistress clapped her hands. 'Put down your work and go out quietly.' There was a general stampede for the door. Two or three stayed on their stools and continued to work.

'Wait for me outside, Nancy. I'll be a minute.' Jane turned to the mistress, a thin, humourless woman in an old brown gown. 'Mrs James, I thought you were supposed to make time for the reading.'

The woman folded her arms and glared at Jane. 'Do you think I have time? There are twenty-nine children here and more to come. I've to spend all my time on the straw, what with the mothers insisting that their girls finish a set length every day.' She looked over to the remaining girls. 'And they have to stay till they've done it. The most I can do is get them to recite a verse of two from the Bible. If you want book learning, send them to the reading school.'

That was not an option, and Jane knew it. 'I would very much like my children to read,' she murmured.

The mistress gave a mirthless laugh. 'Surely you realise that round here the plaiting is more important than education.'

'It seems so,' replied Jane as she turned to go.

CHAPTER 3

Jane had been shocked by the squalor of the plait room. Rebecca had learnt her skill there but at that time there had been fewer children. When Nancy started at four years, Rebecca had taken her sister to school so Jane had no occasion to visit the place at all. Now, the room was overcrowded and filthy. Twenty-nine children sat in a space roughly twelve feet square, unventilated and unheated in winter. They had to work for long hours on a stool, hardly able to move while the two-year-olds crawled around on the floor. It was no wonder they were all pale and had frequent colds and stomach problems, for they looked half starved. And how was Stevie expected to thrive in such a place?

Jane thought back to her own childhood and the clean room and short hours back in Hertfordshire with her own parents. Until he died, herr father had been a strict man but intent on some education for his daughter. As she grew, part of each evening was spent at a reading school, for her father had been a teacher and education was important. He had even taught her a little himself and had ambitions for her. When promotion often took him away from home, she was left with her mother who was not well. Looking after her controlled every aspect of her daughter's life just as Jane was aching to spread her teenage wings. When the tuberculosis took her mother, Jane was lost and now an orphan with no relations to fall back on. At sixteen she was too green to withstand the plait dealer's blandishments.

When Dan came along, she wanted to marry him. She was just eighteen then. He was only a farm worker but she loved him and a life with him would be better than the life she had then.

Outside, the children were waiting. Nancy held Stevie and Dody by the hand but there was no sign of Joey.

'Where is he?

Stevie piped up. 'He said he's going round to the privy for a piddle, Ma.'

Jane lifted her eyes to the heavens. They waited a minute or two then began to walk slowly down the path to home. They soon caught up with Joey, sauntering along, whacking at the hedgerow with a stick.

When they reached home and made for the path to their door, Nancy ran forward. She had seen a wooden crate under the porch. 'Look Ma, someone has left us something.'

Jane hurried to look. The box contained a large turnip, a round firm cabbage, four apples and a piece of bacon. There was no sign who had left the box. She called to Rebecca. 'Who left this, Beccy? Did you see?'

Rebecca looked wide-eyed at her mother. 'No, Ma. I didn't know it was there. I was here all the time except when I went round the back. I think I heard a cart go by when I was in the privy but I didn't see nothin' nor no one.'

'Did you not notice the box when you came back in?'

Rebecca lowered her eyes. 'No, Ma, I was keen to get back to the plaitin'.'

Jane thought immediately of Jethro. She had told him of the fine when beside him on the way home and he must have guessed they would be grateful for the gift of food. He would have had easy access to such an abundance as this. 'Take the box indoors, children,' she said, smiling to herself.

That evening they ate well on the bacon and the apples, leaving the remainder for the Sunday. After Stevie was asleep in the daybed, they put together all the plait completed that day and measured it between the two notches cut a yard apart on the shelf over the fire. Allowing for a visit to St Peter's on Sunday, if they worked hard all the hours of daylight there would be more than one score to sell on Monday.

The market took place in the open air on George Street. Boards, stalls and trestles were set up along the road, loaded with bundles of plait for sale, brought in from the surrounding hamlets and villages by the dealers and the plaiters. There were heaps of bundles of straw, cut into lengths and tied in bundles for sale to the women and the few men not employed in the fields.

Jane arrived after the bell for the start of business was rung at nine o'clock, and the walk had tired her. Already the street was heaving with people and loud with the voices of buyers complaining of short measure and women complaining of the low price they were offered for their handiwork. Dealers inspected the fineness of their work, deciding the quality and price, entering details in their notebooks. They then carried off what they had bought to the hat manufacturers' warehouses in the town. Women queued, their plait held in impatient arms, and Jane pushed her way through the crowds until she found an agent she thought would give her a good price, reminding herself to buy extra bundles of splints, ready bleached and dyed, for the next week's work. On the way, she felt rough hands clutch at her arm and turning, she came face to face with Silas Roberts.

'So you've decided to go it alone, have you, Jane Chapman? We're gonna see how long that lasts. You won't live long on the miserable bunch you've got there.' He nodded at the coils she held.

Pulling her arm free, she stepped back. 'You leave me be, Silas Roberts. I can manage without your interference.'

He guffawed, opening his mouth, revealing brown stained teeth. 'So you gonna walk 'ere Mondays from now on? That little gal of yourn told me as much. She's a bit o' jam, ain't she, quite saucy in 'er way. But you be sure, there ain't no other dealer musclin' in on my patch that would risk 'avin' his eye put out, so you ain't got no option but me, an' that's how it should be, bein' as you and me is almost related.' He hooked both his thumbs in the pockets of his waistcoat and pushed out his bulging stomach and laughed again.

Disgusted by the brazen cheek of the man, the nerve after what he had done to her, Jane looked briefly at his pudgy fingers, his fat belly and his hardened drinker's face, and she turned and walked away, soon lost in the crowds. This was not the place to give vent to her fury with him. But when had Roberts talked to Rebecca? He must have called at the cottage after she had left but she had not seen him on the road. Was her daughter safe, left alone at home with people like him about? She was still only a child but Roberts was capable of anything. Perhaps she should bring Rebecca to the market with her but then the time for plaiting would be even shorter.

Weighed down by this thought, she stood in rank until able to negotiate a reasonable price and tucking the money into her bodice she made her way home. She had only gone a short distance when a familiar cart drew up alongside.

'Get up, Jane, I guessed you'd be comin' about now.'

This time Jane did not hesitate. 'Thank you, Jethro. I'm so pleased to see you. I need to get home quickly.' Sitting beside him, aware of his male closeness, she tried to push such thoughts out of her mind and they travelled in silence. Soon, however, she said, 'Do I have you to thank for the vegetables?'

He flicked the reins but didn't look at her. 'My Da agreed when I told him of the fine. He suggested we help out.'

'I'm very grateful, only Roberts called and I guessed it couldn't be him.' Jethro gave a snort of agreement. 'Watch out for that fellow. I've heard things. These straw dealer fellows are a might too fly these days.'

Jane nodded. 'You don't have to tell me.' At least today she knew where Silas was. After the market he would be in the Lilley Arms, drinking and congratulating himself on a profitable morning, no doubt, and Rebecca would be safe from him.

They continued in silence until Jethro coughed and said, 'I can give you a lift most Mondays, you know.'

'That's very kind, Jethro, but I don't want to put any obligation on you.'

'If you aren't going to deal with Roberts, Luton market is the closest and I go early to sell our own stuff, eggs and that. I usually come back about this time.'

She looked at him and smiled. 'Well, if you come by, I'll be very grateful but if not, then I'll walk. Thank you.' They looked at each other and smiled. 'And thank your father for his kindness. Once I've paid this fine, we should be back to normal. I guess it will be hard going but there's a couple of months before the winter sets in.'

'Ah, the winter. There'll be less work on the farm and there will be free time I could use. I was thinkin' your little garden needs the soil turning over.'

Jane gave a rueful laugh. 'You are right. Daniel was good in the garden but I don't have the time. It's gone to rack and ruin.'

Their small plot behind the cottage was a sorry sight. When Daniel was alive he had grown potatoes, turnips, carrots, and green stuff for the growing family.

'I could dig it over, if you're willing. Then in the Spring you could plant a few vegetables. Save you money, wouldn't it?'

'Would you do that?' She turned to face him, taking the opportunity to gaze freely at the face which lately had figured often in her thoughts. 'That would be very kind of you but you'll soon have everyone wanting your service.'

'They'll be unlucky then,' he swiftly replied.

Jane sat in silence for a while thinking over the offer. It was true times were going to be very hard and truthfully, she did need some help. It would hurt to turn Jethro away and why should she? He was just being neighbourly, wasn't he? She said, 'I would be glad of that, Jethro, but only if your Da agrees and you're not wanted on the farm.'

'Right, it's a deal.' And they smiled again at each other.

CHAPTER 4

When Jane had married, it had not been a pleasant surprise to discover that she had to deal with Silas Roberts, as her mother had done. She had hoped never to see him ever again. He, however, had been jubilant and soon let her know the intervening years made no difference to him. He expected to pick up from where he imagined they had left off. For a long time his appeals were muted for fear of her husband but when Dan died, all restraint was cast aside and he increased his attentions, supposing her to have left off her grieving after a too short period of time. He had offered help 'if she would be obliging'. The wheedling tone told her all she needed to know and her stomach had churned at the idea.

'Come on, Jane, remember me? I'm your sweetheart, ain't I and I'm not askin' much. You need a man after all this time and by rights it should be me.'

'No, never. You've got no rights in me. I've told you that before. Forget it. I'll not be taken advantage of again by you or anyone.'

'But I can 'elp you along and it looks to me like you need it.'

'Not from you, I don't.' Her voice was low and bitter.

'What's the use of playin' hard to get when your kids are one step away from the workhouse?' His voice had hardened. Jane remembered his quivering jowls, the jutting chin. 'You berrer think on what would 'appen if you refuse me.'

She had laughed in his face which had not gone down well. 'Too late, Silas Roberts. I'm not a child any more.'

He had gone away, blurting out for all to hear, 'Who do you think you are?' Since then he had tried his own brand of persuasion, a mixture of ridicule and threats, cajoling and wheedling every Monday morning for the last two years. There had been one occasion not long ago, when she discovered what a dangerous man he was. It had been an afternoon when she was alone in the cottage. He called to buy her plait, doing the rounds of the village, finally thumping on her door. He was in a foul mood, saying he was losing patience with her uppity ways and why did she think she was so special.

Her response was equally unfriendly, in contrast to her usual composure. He had pushed his way over the threshold and pressed her against the table, and proceeded to fumble his way into her skirts. Furiously, she fought this onslaught and despite his greater strength pushed him off her.

'Rape, is that your way of doing business?' she screamed at him. She was sitting on the table, her skirt awry and with her right boot she kicked out, catching him in the groin. He backed off, his face crumpled with pain and fury. 'You're a wildcat, Jane Chapman. You'll be sorry for this.'

'No, I won't. And I'll do the same again if you try it on with me.' Roberts retreated that time, mumbling abuse.

After that assault Jane made sure that Stevie was always with her, supposing that his presence would protect her. By the time he started at the plait school, Rebecca was plaiting at home and her presence was even more effective but Jane could tell from the dealer's many comments that he still harboured his revolting plans. The court case was his latest warped attempt to persuade her.

The rest of the week was going to be an awful time. There was little money for food or any of their necessities except bundles of straw. Day after day they sat together and plaited, hungry and not talking. The small amount that Nancy earned at the school went to pay for her and Stevie's continued attendance, but she needed him to be out from under her feet. By Wednesday she was desperate, with five more days to go and no sign of two pounds in the tin on her shelf over the fire.

Either by design or accident, Jane saw more of Jethro in the coming days. He was the only one to offer help and the thought of him made her days bearable. In her bed at night, thoughts of him brought her comfort. He knew she was struggling and called one evening at her door. Her heart gave a jolt when she saw him standing on her step holding a large marrow and a canister of milk. He held them out.

'Not much, but it will help. A present from Betsy.'

Jane took the things from him. 'Who is Betsy?'

'One of our cows.'

Despite herself, she had to laugh. 'Come in. At least I have tea.'

'Better not. I'm supposed to be cutting hedges. I just want to say that I can find two pounds for you if you'll take it. You can pay the fine on Monday next, and knowing how proud you are, if you want to pay me back you can, but you don't have to hurry doing it.' All this came out in the rush of one breath. He stood looking down at her with anxiety in his eyes.

'Oh Jethro, where can you manage to get that much all at once?'

He turned away to look over to the lane where his horse waited. 'Never mind that.' He paused. 'I will borrow it from my Da.'

'Why should you do that for me?'

'Well, I'd like to help and he won't miss it. He's doing alright this year and he owes me years of back wages.'

Jane stared at him for a long moment. He seemed discomfited. He was at risk of offending his father. She couldn't let him do this. 'I can't take it, Jethro. Your father would not like it.'

'He won't know. But if he did he wouldn't mind. I know he thinks well of you.'

'It feels too much like stealing from him, Jethro. I can't let you do that, no matter how desperate I am.' Two alternatives fought within Jane: gratitude at his determination to help and anguish at the seriousness of her plight. If only there was something he could do for her that wouldn't have bad results. She hung her head to hide her distress. 'I have only one option left to me.'

Out of her desperation Jane had been thinking for some time that she must smother her pride and make a claim to the Poor Law Guardians for help. That was their job. The shame of 'going on the Parish' made her insides curl but she must steel herself to do it. Jane's links were all with Luton, the town she knew best, but Lilley was in Hertfordshire and she knew their Poor Law was administered from Hitchin. But how would she travel there to make her appeal?

'You don't mean to go on the Parish. Anything would be better than that.'

'I must appeal to the Guardians, Jethro, or we will be in the Workhouse by the end of next week even if somehow I can pay the fine. Things are so bad but if I can get to the Union office in Hitchin, I will do my best to persuade them.' She held her hand up to her face in an attempt to hide from him the shame she would have to bear.

The concern he was feeling was clear to see. 'What will you ask for?'

'A loan of the two pounds and some extra for food. Distasteful as it is to ask for charity it is the Union's job to help.' She tried to smile at him but it was a wan effort.

Without hesitation he said, 'If you are determined then I will take you. We must go tomorrow. I'll call in the morning.'

Weak with relief and gratitude, Jane was still for a long moment. 'Would you do that for me, Jethro? You are a true friend. But could you get away? It will take a whole morning. Your father….'

'Don't worry about him. Leave him to me.' He gave her a long lingering look, his brown eyes searching hers, as if there was more to say but this was not the time. Jane reached out and touched his arm in response and the charge thrilled them both. Then he turned abruptly, swung up onto the horse and cantered away.

CHAPTER 5

True to his word, Jethro took Jane to Hitchin the next
morning, the road busy with carts and people. Jane
barely noticed the sun filtering through the early mist
over the fields and when they arrived on the outskirts of
the town, he let her down outside the Poor Law Union
headquarters. In an upper room she found two men, the
elected Guardians, behind a table. Others like herself
waited in another room for their turn but she had
benefited from an early arrival and stood in front of the
gentlemen sporting their fine waistcoats and gold pocket
watches. Who were these supposedly worthy men who
were there to help people like her?

To begin with she was questioned closely on her
circumstances while a substantial form was completed
with her replies. Then the pens were lowered and the
men sat back, examining her clothes, her general mien,
presumably deciding just how indigent she was.

'Now, Mrs Chapman, you are clearly not destitute. Why have you come to us?'

Any hope of avoiding mentioning the fine disappeared at a stroke. There was nothing for it but to own up. 'Sir, I have a debt that must be paid by next week and I cannot earn enough to save my family from the Workhouse.'

'What is this debt?'

'A fine, Sir. I was wrongly accused and the magistrate took against me.'

'How so?'

'He believed my accuser, Sir.'

'So you have been found guilty of a crime.'

'Sir, I would have paid the fine if I could, even though I was innocent of the charge.'

The men smirked at one another and muttered a few quiet words. Then they nodded and turned to her. 'Mrs Chapman, you are able-bodied and therefore the rules disallow our help, especially as you are guilty of a misdemeanour.'

Jane's heart sank and, near to tears, she slumped into the chair beside her that pride had not allowed her to use. There was a pause as the men watched her disappointment. One man said, 'Mrs Chapman, have you applied for an extension to your fine?'

'No, Sir,' Jane murmured.

'Then that is what we recommend you do. We will allow you five shillings to see you through the week but we do not expect to see you before us again.' They recorded the amount on the form and slowly counted out the coins while Jane gathered her thoughts. Despair had given way to anger. All the way to Hitchin to be dismissed in five minutes. These men had no idea how difficult her life was, no idea what poverty meant to those who trailed daily in front of their self-righteous noses.

The interview was at an end. Jane wearily rose, took the money without a word more and left the room. Outside in the street she stood immobile, transfixed by many emotions; regret, shame, and a sense of being robbed of her self-respect. She felt diminished while the busy world carried on around her. Soon Jethro came by, but seeing her expression, said nothing.

Back home at last, Jane was comforted by the thought that now at least they could eat – bread, lard and tea – but the fine still hung over her head. Such was her anxiety, she could not control the trembling in her limbs. She needed the solid comfort that she now believed Jethro would give her, but she guessed he would not come. His father was likely to be angry because of the morning's lost work. Perhaps Jethro had to make up the time. She was racked by a fever of anxiety about what would happen on Monday if she did not arrive to pay the fine. Would they send the constables? What possible arrangements could she make for the children if they came to take her away? Silvie? Jessie? Please God, not Jessie. The children would be taken to the Workhouse for sure. Why had she let Jethro's offer slip away? It had been her pride, her independent nature that had been the stumbling block.

As she paced the room, she saw Rebecca at the table gnawing her fingers, her face a mask of worry. What was she doing to her children? What sort of mother was she? At last, in a shaky voice she asked Rebecca to go to the shop. 'Buy potatoes, Beccy,' she said. 'At least we can afford those.' She noticed the girl's hand trembled as she took the few pence Jane gave her, refusing to look at the feverish, over-bright eyes of her mother.

Running from the house Rebecca almost collided with the stout figure of Silas Roberts on their path. He turned to call as she swept by. 'Don't hurry back, girly. I want to talk to your ma.'

Jane glared at him as he approached, the source of all her trouble. 'What do you want today of all days?'

'I knows what day it is. Thought you might be in need of a loan. Get you outta trouble. Think of it as a little gift.'

'What? You bastard, so that was your plan. Well, you can piss off. I'm taking nothing from you, do you hear? Nor am I in the mood to talk to you.'

'When are you ever?' he said, elbowing his way past her into the room before she could stop him.

'Hey, what do you think you are doing?' she cried, the thumping of her heart suddenly loud in her chest.

'I is gettin' fed up with waitin' for yer, darlin'.' He grabbed her arm.

Jane wrenched it free and backed away, her alarm clear in her pale face. The scent of drink on his breath nauseated her.

'Time to remind you again of your promise. How many more years are yer expectin' me to wait, eh?' He was moving unnervingly close to her, forcing her to step backwards.

'Keep back. I don't want anything from you and I've nothing to give you, that's for sure.'

'Now, now, let's not get hoity toity. You's a woman alone and you knows I'm the man for you.'

Jane studied him, struggling to stay as calm as she could. Could she divert his attention from what he had in mind? 'Look, sit here at the table and we'll talk about it.'

'Ah, now we're gettin' somewhere. Luckily, I's got the time.' He grinned and sat.

Opposite him, she swallowed, forcing herself to breathe slowly and asked, 'How many plaiters do you visit every Monday?'

'Waddya wanna know for? I does all this village on a Monday,' he said, eyeing her with suspicion. 'Hitchin on Tuesday, Dunstable on Wednesday, Hemel Thursday and Tring on Friday, oh, and Toddington on Saturday.'

'And do you visit women in all these places?'

'What do you mean? They is all women.'

'No, I mean compliant women, women who let you in and give you what you want whether they want it or not.'

He looked at her coyly from under his brows. 'Some knows which side their bread's buttered. I don't get no trouble from most, not like you.'

'Do you tell them all they are your best girl?'

'What you gettin' at, Jane Chapman?'

'Just askin',' she said, trying her best to look innocent. 'Only if you've got lots of women, why do you want one more?'

'Ah, but you and me's got an agreement, ain't we? We's on a permanent footing, so to speak. An' you always tell me no, so I wants you all the more.'

'Well, sorry Silas, but nothing doing, not ever. There's no agreement and there never was so you can forget it.'

He jumped up and stood in front of her. 'Why you play these games with me? I won't have no more of it. You knows what I want and I mean to 'ave it.'

Jane's skin prickled with anxiety. He leaned over the table, pulled the cap from her head and threw it aside. She stood to push him away but he had looped his fingers through her hair, pulling her round close to him. Spittle ringed his mouth and the smell of him turned her stomach. He pushed her back across the table, put his other arm against her throat and pushed her down.

Pinned down and unable to cry out, her fearful eyes looked at the rough red face looming above her.

'You've messed me about once too often. Why don't you jus' lie back an' enjoy this? After one time the rest is easy.' He fumbled among her clothes, using his weight to hold down her legs. 'An' this time we'll 'ave no kickin'.'

But Jane's arm was free and reaching up, she grabbed his ear and tugged, loosening the weight of his arm across her throat as he pulled back. She gasped and, releasing his ear, she used both fists to beat his face and chest.

He only laughed. 'You's a little wild cat, aren't yer. Tha's what I like. Don't want things too easy.'

They struggled, deaf to any other sounds. He grabbed her leg, pulled it aside and leaned into her. Her fear made her fight more frantically. He was having difficulty finding a way through all her skirts and petticoats. She heard her muslin blouse tear. There was a chill on her bare skin almost to her waist. For a few moments they struggled even as her strength was failing.

Suddenly the door crashed open and Jethro rushed to Roberts. He grabbed him by the collar and pulled him off Jane. Then he punched Roberts hard on the side of his head. Silas, a man heavy with the flesh of many hours in the tavern, of dissipation and loose living, fell like a stone to the floor.

Jethro pulled Jane up from the table and folded her in his arms. Her hair was in disarray, her breasts were all but bare and her face was red and wet with tears. 'Oh, dear sweet man, thank God you came,' she spluttered.

'Shh,' he whispered and held her until the sobs subsided. Then he fetched her shawl and wrapped it around her, whispering, 'I asked Beccy to stay outside. Can she come in now?'

'What? Oh yes, but can you get this brute outside of here first?'

'Help me, then, if you can. He's heavy.'

Together they dragged the unconscious body of Roberts outside and left him against the house wall where Rebecca was anxiously standing. The girl stood looking down at him, perhaps waiting for some movement, but he was out cold. Jethro and Jane went back inside but she stayed looking down at him for a few minutes then followed them indoors. Jethro was explaining how he came to be near at the critical moment.

'I was coming down the track when Beccy came rushing up to me. She was all out of breath. *It's my ma, Jethro,* she said. *Mr Roberts is at the house and he's hurting her.*'

'I asked her to explain. She said, *He's got her on the table and he's torn her blouse and I think he's trying to kill her.*'

'You said that?' Jane turned quickly to her daughter and pulled her close.

'I thought he was, Ma. I looked through the window and I saw him over you. I banged on the door but I couldn't get in. I went to get Jethro to help.'

Jethro continued. 'Luckily I was so close and I knew it wasn't murder he had in mind.'

They could hear groans from outside the door so Jethro went out to find Roberts trying to stand. Jethro pulled him to his feet. 'Listen to me, you lecherous bastard, if I get one hint of you trying this on again, I shall hunt you down and give you the biggest thrashing of your life. Do you hear me?'

Silas said nothing but growled his fury. Already the side of his face was swollen and bruised. He pulled himself free then staggered away to his horse and cart, a short way down the lane.

Jane was questioning Rebecca. 'Why did you come back, Beccy?'

'I was worried, Ma. I was half way to the shop but I turned round 'cos I don't trust him.'

'Oh, my lovely girl.' Jane hugged her thanks and kissed her many times. 'What would I do without you?'

Watching them, Jethro unfolded his arms and took his leave. 'Are you sure you are alright, Jane? I was bringing you some vegetables but I dropped them in the garden. I'll call back later if that's alright.'

When they were alone, Rebecca took three pound notes from her pinafore pocket and held them out to her mother. 'I took them from Mr Roberts, Ma. They were sticking out of his pocket as he was lying outside.'

Jane was astounded and looked at the notes with wonder and relief on her face.

'There was lots more but I only took three. Two for the fine and one for luck. Was it stealing, Ma?'

'I suppose so, but let's not worry about that. I reckon he owes us, don't you?' And she fetched the tin from the shelf and tucked the notes inside.

CHAPTER 6

It was as if a fresh breeze had blown through the cottage, such was the joy and relief they all felt. Even when the little 'uns came home from the school, they caught the atmosphere. The fine could be paid on Monday and there was food for supper. No potatoes, of course, but they enjoyed Jethro's other more nourishing gifts. When the children had gone to bed and the house was quiet, Jethro tapped on the door.

'I've brought a spade,' he said. 'I'll make a start on your garden. I have an hour while Da's at the Lilley Arms. He goes to play cribbage and gambles a little some nights. How are you feeling?'

'A lot better than if you had not arrived when you did. I'm so grateful, Jethro. What a state I would be in now if he had succeeded in his wicked plan.'

'You must stay out of his way, Jane. Don't deal with him if you can help it.'

'Not so easy, I'm afraid. He's the only dealer in this village. But I will walk to Luton now if I have to and avoid him completely.'

'Then I will take you every Monday to keep you safe from him. You can rely on me.'

Jane gazed up into his determined face. 'I can't expect you to do that for me.'

'Don't you realise by now that I would do anything in the world for you, Jane?'

His words stopped Jane's breath. She was hearing words that she never dreamt she would hear. Did he feel as she did? She reached out and tentatively put hand on his cheek, feeling the rough skin beneath her fingers, hoping the gesture would stand in for the words she dare not say. He took hold of the hand and brought it to his lips.

Jane was overcome and took a step closer, feeling the warmth of him as his arms went round her and pulled her closer still. 'Oh my dear, I did so hope…' she muttered.

'So did I, but I did not dare to speak. For such a long time the sight of you has gladdened me.'

She shook her head in disbelief. 'Is that so? And you gave me no sign.'

'Then now is the time to make up for that.' And he pulled her even closer and kissed her fiercely as if all the pent-up longing of the past flooded through him.

They stood intertwined for several long moments, then trembling, Jane stepped back. 'Come and sit and we can talk. Shall I make tea?'

'Let me do some of the garden first.'

'If you must,' she said, smiling shyly at him.

When she closed the door, she looked around the room and joyfully tidied away the litter of the day, the straw cuttings on the floor, the tin plates of their meal still in the basin and the chemise and nightgowns drooping over the line from the beams.

It was quite dark when she heard his gentle tap on the door and she let him in. He sat at their table while she made tea. They were shy with each other until Jane spoke to fill the silence. 'It must be hard work out there. No one has touched the garden since Dan died.' There was a tension in the air and they both felt it.

'It'll take a while.'

She sat opposite him with the two mugs of tea and they whispered together lest Stevie woke.

'Luckily the garden is hidden from my neighbours.'

He nodded.

'Was your father angry that you took me to Hitchin? Is that why you didn't come on Friday?'

The last words came out in a rush and she lowered her eyes to the table. He reached over and took hold of her hands. 'He was none too pleased. Someone else had to do my chores and the cart was missing. He was keen to know where I had been so I told him. That shut him up. Best if we keep Mondays secret and I'll come after my day's work to do the garden.'

'But why? He's usually keen to help anybody. He's always been nice to me.'

'Yes, I think that's the problem.' He frowned down at the table and didn't reply when she asked him what he meant.

They sat thinking for a long moment, their hands touching. They smiled at each other and Jane wondered what she should say to fix this moment in her heart. Instead, he spoke.

'I wish...'

'What do you wish, Jethro?' She could see he was struggling to frame a reply.

'I wish you were mine.'

His words both shocked and delighted her. Such courage, she thought, her eyes glinting in the candlelight. She gazed into his eyes. 'I have thoughts like that but you are an eligible bachelor and I am a widow with three children. How could you really want me when there are so many younger women in the village'

His expression became thoughtful. 'I know them all and some further afield, silly girls with expectations.

What have I to offer any of them? Anyway, I know what I want.'

'Oh Jethro, could it ever be so?'

He didn't reply but pulled her hands towards his lips and kissed her fingers. The charm and grace of the gesture stirred her heart beyond words. Across the table, their hands tightly entwined, their eyes had to say everything. After a moment, Jethro stood and moved round to her, stood behind and curled his arms around her shoulders while leaning down and pressing his lips to the side of her neck. The thrill of his touch brought every nerve in her body alive and aching for more. He slid his hands over her breasts, then feeling the eagerness he found there, he slid his hands under the fabric of her blouse until his palm felt the hard nipples and his fingers the softness and weight of her breasts. 'Oh,' she cried, overwhelmed by the exquisite response that flooded through her whole body. She twisted on the chair and raising her arms, she reached high to place them round his neck, pulling him down so that they could kiss and acknowledge the desire surging through them both.

They could go no further. The children lay sleeping not yards away, and might wake at any moment. The quiet of the room was sure to be broken if they allowed free rein to the passion that gripped them. They had to pull apart. Jethro returned to his seat and Jane did her best to control her trembling limbs and hands. They talked softly, nonsense talk, each thrown awry by the wonder of the sensations coursing through them, until Jethro said he had better go, promising to come again as soon as he could.

Jane walked with him to the door and as she raised the latch, he put his arm round her waist and pulled her close. For a moment her head rested on his shoulder and she breathed his male smell, and felt his hands on her, so long wished for. She looked up into the dark hollows of his eyes. 'Come again, Jethro,' she murmured. He stepped back.

'Just try and stop me,' he murmured, then she had to let him go.

Chapter 7

Sunday was the day when they went to St Peter's in the morning and took a picnic up to Ward's Wood if the weather was good enough. It made a break from all the hours spent cooped up in the school or spent plaiting at home. To be out in the fresh air allowed the children to run about and play among the trees or in the stream close by. The water ran clear and icy cold over the chalky bottom and they took off their boots and paddled, then ate a picnic of bread and cheese while Jane sat on the verge, busy with the plaiting she had brought with her.

With the fine no longer a problem and remembering the bad air in the plait room and Rebecca's furious efforts to do her utmost to help her mother, Jane thought their walk was more necessary than usual. The track passed the entrance to Ward's farm. As they passed by, they were hailed by Arthur Ward. He left the heap of manure he was shovelling and came to the gate.

'Afternoon, Jane. You goin' up the wood again? I see you most Sundays.'

She walked over towards him. 'I hope Jethro gave you my thanks for the vegetables and the bacon.'

'Aye, he did, but I was glad to give 'em. He tells me he took you to Hitchin.'

'I was grateful for that too, but much good it did me.'

'I heard that too. It's back to the plaiting then, but you're a good worker, like your Dan. We miss him sorely, we do.'

Jane was not happy to be reminded of Dan so she forced a smile, and turned to go. She liked Arthur, a well-built man of about fifty. He had a full head of hair, now white at the temples and his face was weathered but carried a pleasant expression at all times as far as she could tell.

The day Dan died he had come to her door and, leaning on the threshold like a man distraught, had told her that Dan was dead. It was not his fault and he could not be blamed but he took it almost as badly as she did.

It was only later that she was able to absorb the details and even now she could not bear to remember. No one knew how it had happened but something had startled the mettlesome horse, and rearing up, it had tipped the cart, throwing Dan to the ground and a load of rocks on top of him.

It was a grief-stricken time after that. People were kind and the vicar buried Dan at no cost in the tiny churchyard. Jane had lost her man, her breadwinner, and had to fall back on the plaiting. Arthur Ward had lost his best worker and did all he could to help but all these things tailed off after a while. After all, Jane was not the only woman to lose a husband or a son to an accident at work.

Arthur Ward was watching sorrow flit over Jane's face. 'You're a good woman, Jane, one of the best round here. If there is any more I can do for you, you have only to say.'

Jane smiled feebly and lowered her eyes. 'I have to learn to manage, but thank you.'

As they walked on along the track, she wondered if his seeing them most Sundays meant anything. Was he keeping a look out for her and if so, why should he do that? Perhaps he felt some guilt over Dan's death. She hoped not, for he was not responsible for what happened and had nothing to make up for.

What had Jethro meant by '*I think that's the problem*'? Arthur Ward was always kind but perhaps he had something against her that made secrecy necessary? Was it because she was a widow with children? Was she too poor and dependent? She and Jethro were both single so there was no real impediment to the relationship, but perhaps he had some other reason to think her an inappropriate mate for his son.

When they reached the wood, they decamped by the stream. Jane pulled out her plaiting. 'Go wash in the stream, dears. Rebecca, keep an eye on Stevie while you wash.'

Before them, the sunlight filtered through the foliage on to the grass and the trees behind sheltered them from the chill of the breeze. Soon the children's joyful voices rang out as they played. They were eating their food when a crunching of twigs in the trees behind them alerted Jane to someone approaching. She looked round, delighted to find Jethro making his way towards them. He was carrying a bundle of wire and string that she recognised as rabbit snares. She smiled up at him.

'Poaching today, are you?'

'It's not poaching on your own land,' he laughed and sat down on the grass beside her.

'I'm so pleased to see you, Jethro.' She groped for his hand in the grass.

'I hoped you'd be here.' His eyes slid from hers to her lips and then further, to her throat, her breasts.

'We saw your father on the way here. We talked a bit. He was pleasant with no hint of resentment at your helping me.'

'Well, he wouldn't. It was me he was angry with.'

'Because of taking time away from the farm? Not because it was me?'

'I don't think he's too happy with the idea of you and me... you know.'

'But why? What's wrong with me?'

'Nothing. That's the problem.'

'You said that before but I don't understand.'

Jethro sighed deeply and pulled at the grass at his other side. 'He's lonely, Jane. It's five years since my mother died and he's tired of coping alone. You are the best there is in these parts and I believe he's got plans. If he thought that you and I were getting close, well, I don't know what he would do.'

Jane suddenly became very still. She gave a slow disbelieving shake of her head. What could she make of this news, if it was true? She stuttered, 'But I can't... I couldn't... I never would...'

'That is why I say we must meet in secret.' Deep in the grass, she felt his grip tighten. The children were moving close enough to hear what they were saying so there was no further chance to ask how long they must hide how they felt about each other or what the end point could possibly be.

He was so close. Jane felt the heat of him and smelled the mown hay smell of his skin. There were beads of sweat on his brow that he swept away with a brusque hand. His forearm was tanned but she noticed the fine brown hairs where his shirt sleeves were rolled. His face was strong with a well-shaped jaw, deep-set eyes, and lips that she longed to kiss.

'You'd best go, Jethro, or he might ask where you've been. He knows we come here on a Sunday.'

He groaned and stood, slowly gathering the wire coils. 'I'm setting traps for the pot and he knows it, but still…' He touched her lightly on the shoulder and began to walk back into the trees.

Jane waited a while before she called the children to her and they too began the walk home.

The next morning, market day, was a chance to both pay the fine and add to what remained of her five shillings in the tin Jane kept on the shelf over the fire. Winter was approaching and in the morning they all woke to an early autumn frost. Jane went out before the children were up to collect some cut gorse, fallen branches and twigs to light the fire and warm the place. Rebecca would have to look after the fire while Jane was off to Luton with their scores of plait and the two pounds safely in her pocket. It would be a burden lifted, but there was still no reason to relax their labours. They had measured their work against the notches on the shelf and Jane was hopeful that because of their long hours all day and late into the evening, straining their eyes in the gloom, she could get a better price than Roberts had given. Her mouth and Rebecca's were sore and cracked from the unremitting softening of the straw as they moistened it between their lips.

As soon as the children were up, she instructed Beccy to give them a breakfast of bread and treacle and see them off to the school. 'Then you must close the door and open it for no one until I get back. Do you understand?'

Rebecca nodded. 'Shall Nancy call for Joey and Dody?'

'Yes, of course. A penny halfpence is better than none.'

Nancy called from the window. 'Ma, Jethro has stopped outside. Has he brought us something?'

Jane grabbed her shawl and the bundles of plait. 'No, dear, he'll give me a lift to the market to save time.' She kissed them all briefly and hurried out.

'I'm on my way early, Jane. Hop up and we'll make good time.'

She wished Jethro a good morning and climbed up beside him. 'I'm so grateful to you. You are a fair sight on such a cold morning.' Her eyes sparkled with gratitude.

'You are a sight for my eyes too,' he observed, as she tucked the loose curls escaping from beneath her muslin cap and pulled her shawl over her shoulders.

'If I am early, maybe I'll make more money,' she said. 'I will be so glad to put this time behind us. Beccy is panicking and plaiting furiously and I can't stop her although her fingers are almost cut raw.'

'She's a grand lass, and quick too. I guess she was afraid you wouldn't be able to pay the fine.'

'It's thanks to her that I can. She's heard tales of the Workhouse and the thought scares her.'

They rode on in silence. Jane smiled to herself as they passed Jessie's cottage and saw her gawping as they went by. Jessie didn't go to the market – she sent her two daughters instead to sell their family's work. The girls were at her side ready to go. They were tricked out in their best, with ribbons and dried flowers in their bonnets, supposing that the dealers would respond better to pretty girls than old mothers. That calculation might well be true, thought Jane, because Jessie was a woman made older by her frequent childbearing.

One of the girls called out as the cart passed. 'Got room for two more in yer cart, Jethro? We'll make it worth your while.'

Jane glanced sideways and caught his frown and pursed lips. He pretended not to hear and flicked the reins to encourage the horse.

He dropped her at the edge of the town. 'I've got some errands for my Da but I'll try and catch you on the way back.'

'Thank you, Jethro, but you must do what you have to and don't mind about me.' Once again their eyes locked and a frisson of pleasure went through her. Was it just his strong arms that pleased her, or the shoulders and firm thighs? Surely she should see deeper than that. It was the sense of inner strength he had, his generous nature and his kindness that moved her. He reminded her of Dan when he was younger.

The bell was just ringing as she reached George Street and the business of the day began. Keeping an eye out for Roberts she stood in one of the ranks of women already waiting their turn to sell. Soon Jessie's girls came by, having paid tuppence to a carter to save them the walk. They were giggling and gossiping but when they saw her their heads went together, nodding and whispering, no doubt making much of seeing Jane and Jethro together earlier.

The dealer inspected her scores minutely. Some were of English Wholestraw, a coarse shiny plait that Rebecca had done. She had also managed some English Pearl, a slightly finer and more complicated plait that took the girl more time but was worth more money. Jane's own work was finer still, made with straws split into thinner strips by the strawsplitter Dan had screwed to the back of the door. She also had a score of the Brilliant design and some of English Wave. Each length had been flattened and softened by passing it through their plait mill to make it more pliable.

After his inspection, the dealer looked sharply at her. 'I'll see you again, lady, if you've got as good to sell next time.'

'Then you'll give me a good price for this,' Jane replied eagerly. The man sighed heavily and handed over a good few coins. Pleased, she nodded her satisfaction and turned away.

Jane began the long walk home, stopping only to buy some sixpenny bundles of straw for the coming week. Before long Jethro stopped to pick her up. He too had sold some of the farm's produce to the shops, so with a lighter load the horse trotted briskly and they were soon at the cottage where inside Rebecca was working hard.

'Enough work for now, Beccy. Give your hands a rest. Look what I've got.' She reached into her pinafore pocket and brought out four eggs. 'Jethro gave them for us tea. Now we'll have some of that bacon with bread and butter to be going on with.' She quickly pulled out the money they had earned and added it to the coins in her tin.

A wide smile spread over Rebecca's face and she leaned back and dropped her work. 'Nobody came, Ma, and I only went out the back once.'

'Good, all the world was at the market. I saw Jessie's girls there.'

'The big girls? That's Maisie and Flo.'

Jane thought the two looked flighty and were clearly spending their earnings on fancy clothes. She knew that in the summer they both disappeared into the fields with the local lads and she guessed they were no better than they should be.

Rebecca sat dreamily, her cut fingers resting in her lap. 'I'd like a bonnet like Maisie's. One with a big brim that I can put ribbons and flowers on.'

'One day, my chicken, who knows. But I guess you'll have to move from the village and go to Luton or perhaps Hitchin where the factories are. You'll need to learn new skills. Your Da wanted to better himself but never made it.'

Rebecca put her worst cracked finger into her mouth to sooth it. 'What could I do there, Ma?

'You could do bonnet sewing. There's machines now that can do the work. You could go into service in some big house and taste luxury if you don't mind being a slave. Or there's paper making, cardboard box making for packing hats and bonnets. They go all over the world from here, you know. Then there's silk but I've heard that's as hard as plaiting. There are factories for all these in Luton.'

'I don't fancy any of those except bonnet sewing. I might be good at that.'

'If you can read and write you might even do better but you won't have to think about it until you are much older.'

'I know. But you can read and write, Ma. Why didn't you do something else?'

Jane reached over and sliced a small pat of butter for her bread and paused, then after a moment's thought she said, 'Because I married your father, Beccy.'

CHAPTER 8

'Did you steal 'em, Ma?' Stevie said when he saw the eggs.

His mother frowned. 'No, I did not. He gave them to me. Says he was sorry about your Da, that's why.'

Nancy said, 'Stevie's been listening to the boys, Ma. They was tauntin' us about stealin' plait.'

'Well, next time you tell 'em I'm no thief.'

'Ma, what's a whore?' Stevie said. Jane turned swiftly to her son but when she saw his innocent face, her anger melted. 'Shut up now, and help me coddle these eggs.'

Earlier in the afternoon, before the children came home, there had been a knock at the door. Jane had just stacked the fire with sticks so that they could warm their cold fingers and toes when they came in.

Rebecca opened the door and stepped back in fright when Silas Roberts stood before her. 'I wish to speak to yer Ma, little girl.'

Jane moved quickly to push Rebecca aside. 'Go sit, Beccy. Leave him to me.' To Roberts, she said, 'What do you want?' She looked him over. Clearly he had come from the tavern and was red of face and his words were slurred. 'I have no wish to talk to you.'

'Aw Jane, can't we bury the hatchet, you bein' my best customer and all that. All that nonsense was a misunderstandin', tha's all.'

'That misunderstanding nearly starved us, you bastard, not to mention your attack on me.'

He sighed loudly. 'You's a mighty proud woman, Jane Chapman, considerin' you got nuttin'. I heard you sold to Yates, this mornin'. Up betimes you were. A waste of half a day, I reckon.'

Jane said nothing, but frowned. Clearly he had been checking up on her. There were fat spills from his tavern dinner down the front of his waistcoat. He wiped his stubby fingers repeatedly over the thin hairs on his scalp and on the growth on his jowls that quivered as he stuttered out his words. 'What say you to putting all this business behind us, you and me bein' such old friends?'

Jane raised her eyebrows and was hard put to stifle the screech that rose to her throat. 'How you dare to do what you did and expect me to forget it. You're an animal, Silas Roberts, and I want no more to do with you.'

He had the decency to look shamefaced and fidgeted on her step. 'Aw, Jane, you knows I get a bit roused in me cups. Just got carried away, tha's all. It's your fault for bein' so good lookin'. Yer drive a man wild, yer know. You oughta be flattered.'

'What, flattered? I'll say it again, Silas Roberts, I've done with you. Now get off my step and don't come here again.'

He frowned, determined to the last. 'Come on now, let's pick up where we left off. I'll pick up your plait and save you the walk on a Monday.' He took a step towards her, putting out a hand to the door frame for support. 'Waddya say?'

'Get off my step. We'll manage without your help.'

He drew himself up, a ridiculous but angry glint in his eye. 'I done my best to be fair 'ere. You's too stubborn to see what's best for you. Better watch out 'cos I'm a bad man to cross when my living is threatened.'

'Oh yes, what can you do that's worse than what you've already done?'

He tapped the side of his bulbous nose. 'Well now, I got some mighty persuasive ways up my sleeve.'

'Go away,' Jane said, losing patience with him and she closed the door on his disgruntled face, forcing him to remove his fingers swiftly from the door jamb.

From her seat by the fire, Rebecca called, 'What did he want, Ma?'

'He wants our plait, that's what he wants, but he's not getting it. He'll get nothing from me. I got a better price from Yates. I just hope Jethro can get me there every Monday but I will walk if I have to.'

Taking her tin of coins to the table, Jane counted out the remaining coins. There were enough to see them through the week but it would still be bread and cabbage soup and maybe a slice of turnip until next Monday. 'I want you to run to the shop, Beccy. Buy us some lard and some flour and a little tea if I can have it on tick.' She handed over a few coins. 'I'll make dumplings to go with the eggs.'

Silvie called later in the afternoon, saying, 'I was worried about you. How are things, Jane? Did you manage to pay the fine? I saw you this morning in Jethro's cart. It's kind of him to give you a lift.'

'I'm fine, Silvie and yes, I've paid my debt. Looks like you and everyone else saw me with Jethro. We've got an arrangement since I've sent Silas Roberts on his way.'

'Why, what's he done now?'

'Tried it on again. I only escaped by the skin of my teeth.'

'What a menace. I've heard he tries it on with everyone.'

Silvie didn't ask, so Jane was happy to let her assume the arrangement with Jethro was a financial one. Instead Silvie said, 'I've always liked Jethro. If I hadn't got my Ivor I'd have set my cap on him myself. I know a lot of girls have.' Much good it's done them.'

'I always thought he was shy but I don't think he is.'

'He was very close to his mother, so Ivor says. He was real cut up when she died and since then his Da has kept him on a tight leash. Never lets him leave the farm, I heard and never pays him a penny. He's cheap labour, saving Mr Ward paying any other labourer. I've been expecting him break out any time'

'Really? I thought the farm was doing better than that.'

'Some years bad, some years good, so my Ivor says.

'He's not likely to go for anyone dirt poor, then.'

'Nothing to offer but drudgery on a run down farm, I expect. And if he's stuck there, where is he going to find a wife of any kind?'

Jane chewed her lip. 'Not much point in any of us trying.'

'You could. Why don't you try your luck? You're a fine woman, Jane. He can tell you come from a good family.'

'I must admit I like him a lot. For two years I've never looked at another man. I could not contemplate even the suggestion. I don't know why now is different, but I am rather taken with him.' She had to turn away to hide the blush this understatement caused. 'It's crept up on me because he's so… kind.' She could hardly admit to Silvie that she couldn't get him out of her thoughts.

Silvie gave a hoot and punched Jane gently on the arm. 'Good luck to you, Jane. You deserve to be happy though to my mind, at twenty-six, he is leaving it a bit late.'

'But he is still a young man. Any girl younger, prettier and single might easily tempt him away from me. Our lives are so different, how could I be sure he wasn't just flirting?'

Silvie shook her head. 'I don't think he's that sort of chap, Jane. He's steady and reliable; I'd put money on it.'

When Silvie had gone, Jane thought of this affirmation and her mood lightened. She had been thinking of her talk with Roberts earlier, wondering if they could really manage without him, and it had depressed her. This village was his patch and no other dealer came by. Would it be right to expect Jethro to take her and bring her home every Monday? In the warmer months he would be busy on the farm and she would still have the walk. It would be an obligation put on him and she didn't want to do that. Being dependent on anyone was not to be borne, even Jethro, though he asked nothing of her. If she could not cope with her own problems in this life, then she was weak, and then what kind of mother would she be?

However, there was no one else to help and if they didn't sell plait, they wouldn't eat and would sink even lower into poverty. Her pride and the urge not to be beholden was strong in her, but life was going to be hard. If only for her children she would have to swallow her pride and do what was necessary for them. If she were ever to renew her relationship with Roberts, could she keep him at bay? He was a risk but maybe a risk she might have to take no matter how distasteful it was. These thoughts raced round and round in her mind until the children came in from school and Rebecca returned from the shop.

CHAPTER 9

'Come quick, Jane, Nancy's burned herself with the dicky pot!'

There had been an urgent knocking on the door in the late morning when they were both hard at work. It was Silvie again, her breath coming out as white clouds as she panted. With a cry, Jane grabbed a shawl and made for the door. 'Stay here, Rebecca, don't stop your work.' She rushed out and the girl watched both of them hurry along the road to the school.

The dicky pots were always a danger. Jane knew from her own experience how good it felt to warm your frozen toes on a little pot of embers but she had told the girls again and again not to tuck them under their skirts. Nancy had done what many of the older girls did and bought embers from the baker's fire at a halfpenny a time. If Nancy had burned herself and her mother had been called, it must be a bad burn. Trembling with fear, Jane ran, with Silvie not far behind.

Silvie well understood Jane's panic and had warned her own daughter many times. Burns were common in the winter months, and a child had been known to die of them. Mostly the children held the pots in their laps but the older girls found them more warming under their skirts while they sat for long hours on the cold benches.

There was pandemonium when Jane burst into the room. The children were huddled together against the back wall and Nancy sat hunched on a stool, her face clenched in pain. As soon as she saw her mother she burst into a fresh bout of tears, the girls around doing their best to comfort her.

'Show me,' Jane cried as she knelt before Nancy. The girl leaned forward and pulled the scorched edges of her skirt up to her knees. There were *oohs* and *ahs* from the onlookers. A fierce red weal was revealed, the edges already blistering. Jane's heart thumped. It looked awfully bad.

Jane leaned back on her heels among the cut straw littering the floor, fighting the feeling of helplessness that came over her. Close by was the upturned pot spilling its now cooling ashes around the girls' feet. Jane turned to face the mistress standing by, her arms folded. Anger rose at the sight of the woman's unconcern.

'Why did you allow it? Don't you know the danger by now?'

The woman gave a toss of her head. 'I can't stop them if they pay good money. They need the warmth.'

'But in the skirts?'

'Can't risk staining the plait. That's why they do it.'

Jane knew this was not true. Rebecca had moaned often about the icy, unheated rooms. 'This is your fault!' she cried.

'I can't watch all of 'em every minute. These girls do what they want.'

Jane looked down at the mess of Nancy's leg. There was no point in arguing now when her daughter needed urgent help.

'Silvie, could you fetch the carter? I have to find a doctor, maybe take her to Dunstable.' As Silvie rushed to the door, Jane added, 'Tell him I'll pay when we get back.'

In only a few minutes the carter arrived and Jane carried Nancy out, snatching the mistress's shawl hanging on the back of the door. Nancy was weak and white faced. The pain was severe and each bump in the road as they jolted along made her cry out. Jane wrapped the spare shawl around her and enclosed her tightly in her arms. 'Silvie, look out for Stevie,' she called as they set off.

Jane held her daughter tightly in her arms. She was beset by helplessness and anguish that robbed her of any other concern. After much frantic searching, they reached a doctor's house.

He treated and dressed Nancy's leg, gave Jane instructions on its care and sold her bandages and ointment to sooth and speed healing. By now Nancy was subdued but unable to walk, and had to be carried back to the waiting cart.

It was a late afternoon before they returned home. The cart drew up and Jane carried Nancy into the cottage. The child was white but she smiled feebly, trying to be brave. Stevie was there, brought home by Silvie into Rebecca's care. His face was tear-stained and he was hungry and upset at the turn of events.

Anticipating some likely expense, as Jane had rushed earlier from the house, she had snatched the tin from the shelf and stuffed it into her pinafore. She had paid the doctor and now paid the carter. The now empty tin was replaced on the shelf. The few days of relief were over and they were back to square one.

Rebecca's eyes widened as Nancy lifted her skirt to reveal the long bandage on her right leg. Her skirts were burned, the edges of the fabric scorched and brown.

'You'll not do that again, will you.' Her mother's face was grim. She put a round box of ointment on the shelf.

Rebecca's concern for her sister and her frustration burst out. 'Why are you so stupid? You know how careful you have to be. Now we've got no money left and we'll have to keep on plaiting all over again because of you.'

Her mother turned to her. 'Quiet, Rebecca. She's only six. What's done is done. We'll just have to work harder.'

'But I can't. I can't go any faster.' And she burst into tears.

Jane pulled her close and hugged her. 'I'm sorry Beccy, but we'll manage somehow.'

'Not by giving in to Mr Roberts, Ma. You can't do that.'

Her mother didn't answer but her eyes narrowed and she drew her mouth into a firm line. She looked bleakly around their room. Comfortless and cold, the fire in the grate barely alight, what were they to do? Nancy must now stay at home and even the few pence she might have earned were lost. There would be no let up to their plaiting for the rest of the week. Yes, the fine had been paid but the tin on the shelf was empty. They had rent to pay and they must eat and stay warm. The rent might wait a week, but she would have to buy food on tick and pay the debt at the shop when she could. She looked at her three children, pale and miserable around her. No matter how hard they worked there was no end to the unremitting struggle. Once again the risk of having to go on the Parish loomed.

The two girls were silent. They knew what it meant to go on the Parish. It meant charity. It meant grovelling and not being able to hold your head up and everyone knowing you'd got nothing, that you were as low as dirt under people's feet. The next step was the Workhouse.

Jane fought the despair that overwhelmed her. All they had to last them the week was what Rebecca had bought from the shop. They could plait, for some of the bundles of cut straw were left but there remained only stubs of candle so there was little work they could do after dark when those were gone. Rebecca would take on the chore of looking after Nancy and she was also willing to walk Stevie to the school, along with Joey and Dody. She would call at Jessie's cottage to pick them up and no doubt come back with tales of the erratic habits of their neighbours, of the filth and disgusting sight of their overcrowded home. Jane would still plait hour after hour as before and just hope that the worry would speed her fingers so that the scores coiled in the corner of their room would grow.

When Jethro called after dark, he found Jane preoccupied. She shushed him as he came into the cottage, first leaning his spade against the wall. Jane pointed to the daybed where Nancy was sleeping. 'She can't climb the up to the bedroom so must stay down here. I've had to put Stevie in my bed. He was delighted, of course, but I'm not sure how fast a sleeper Nancy is and her leg hurts. She may wake.'

Jethro looked over to the supine figure. He knew of the accident and now realised the implications of the change. 'Poor girl,' he said but his expression was gloomy. 'Is there nowhere else we can meet?'

Anguished, Jane shook her head. She had been thinking; the fields, the garden? Impossible. 'I can't leave them alone in the house. There's nowhere.' She went to him and held him close, whispering into his ear. 'But it won't be for long. She will heal.'

'I want you so much,' he replied. 'How long do we have to wait?'

'It is so hard, my darling, but we'll just have to be patient.'

How hard patience was. She wanted him and when they embraced she could tell his need was as fierce as hers. Yet in the quiet of the night she told herself that while they held off from that final desired act, she could pull back and allow him to do the same. It wasn't that they were not committed to each other. They talked of it, acknowledged it, made promises, but all the time there was this one last thing that separated them. They were already taking a risk but until the irrevocable final moment, they were innocent. They could say to anyone that their liaison was not serious. It was just a good friendship. So for the time being, they must both bear the joy and the ache of longing at the same time and cope as best they could.

They kissed, they murmured the words all lovers shared and then Jethro went out to dig some more.

CHAPTER 10

The family had no option but to live thriftily on the little they earned until things improved. No further relaxation was possible unless Jethro brought supplies from the farm. As Nancy's leg healed she became irritable. 'I need a new skirt, Ma,' she moaned. 'I can't wear that burnt old thing.'

'We can't afford other clothes yet, Nancy. You'll have to make do.'

Nancy grimaced. 'No one else wears burnt clothes. Why do I have to? I do some plaiting, don't I? Why can't I buy a skirt with my own earnings?'

'Because your earnings go into the pot to feed us, child. Be patient.' Jane lowered her head to her work, ignoring Nancy's sulky expression and stifling the urge to tell her daughter everything was her own fault.

There would be no new skirt for Nancy and the girl really must improve the quality of her plaiting. There would be one penny and a halfpence due from Jessie but lots of straw to buy as well as candles at four pence a pound, soap at thruppence and fuel, if they couldn't collect enough firing themselves. These were necessities, but then there was food: bread, cheese, sugar, oatmeal and salt, and they must have flour and potatoes. From now on they must forgo meat, butter, and tins of treacle unless a gift from the farm came their way.

True to his word, Jethro took her to the plait market every Monday morning and, when he could, brought her home as well. The trip cut out a morning's plaiting, especially when Rebecca was doing a little less. Jane relied on her and worried that she was putting too much responsibility on her daughter but Rebecca didn't complain.

Occasionally, if Jethro could bring some, there was a little meat in their meals, something they had not enjoyed for a long time, and there was tea instead of just water. Over time, despite their privations, the cottage rang with cheerful voices; even Nancy was improving, hobbling out of bed once a day, gritting her teeth in silent sufferance when the bandages were changed.

'Shall we go to the wood, Ma?' Rebecca asked on one Sunday. It was a fine autumn day and although chilly, a fresh breeze blew through the cottage, sweeping away the smell of the tallow candles of the evening before, that always burned with a smoky flame and a strong rancid smell.

'Yes, let's!' cried Nancy, pulling herself up on to one elbow. 'I can make it, really I can. I'm bored with the cottage, and bending over the plait makes my back ache.'

Jane looked at the girls, biting her lip. Nancy was complaining about even the small amount of plaiting she had tried. But she could not walk all the way up the track. It would be good to get out into the fresh air, however.

'Rebecca, go across to Jessie's and ask if we may borrow her hand cart for the day.'

Rebecca soon returned pushing the small cart by its two long handles and Nancy was installed with her blanket about her legs.

Jane put together some food for their picnic. Her patchwork bag used for all her shopping held some bread, some cheese, four apples and some cold dumplings, and a little extra in case Jethro should join them. To this she added a bundle of splints for this was no occasion to stop the plaiting, no matter where they went.

They made slow progress up the track. Rebecca helped Jane as well as she could but it was hard work for young arms. When they approached the entrance to Ward's farm, they stilled their chatter and passed as silently as they could. Jane hoped not to have words with Arthur and checked furtively that he was not in the yard, watching out for them. The children sensed her concern and went quietly by.

When they reached the stream, Nancy tucked up her skirts and limped slowly into the water, hoping that the cool flow would aid the healing as her mother had said.

It was good to be in the fresh air and enjoy a picnic as usual.

After a while, Jethro joined them, two dead rabbits swinging from his belt. He slung them down on the grass and sat down beside Jane.

'Ought you to be here?' she murmured softly, smiling as his arm crept around her waist.

'Ah, you want me to stay away?' he joked, his eyes meeting hers as he leaned back, prompting her to lean forward into him.

'No, no, never, but I was thinking about your father and the risk of him seeing us together.'

'People see us on Mondays – somebody is bound to tell him sooner or later.'

'Yes, but you can say you are just being neighbourly. Shall I pay you for the ride? That should satisfy him, surely.'

Jethro grinned and shook his head, then asked, 'Have you talked to him recently?'

'No, we crept by the farm this afternoon but there was no sign of him.'

'I have a suspicion he's going to call on you.'

'Really? Why should he do that? Do you think he knows something?'

'I've no idea, Jane. He's a mystery to me right now. Ever since I told him I took you to Hitchin, he's been clearing out all my mother's old stuff from the chests where they were mouldering, and making a fuss about mud and mess and saying the house is like a flophouse. He's not usually so finicky.'

'Well, if he wants to help us I'll be glad to see him. Perhaps he knows about the lifts but nothing else. How could he? No one else knows and I certainly am not going to tell him.'

Jethro bit his lip and looked over to where the children were searching in the shallows. 'Your Nancy is healing well. She'll soon be right as rain, won't she? Not so the boy, though.' Jethro looked over to where Stevie was paddling. 'He needs fattening up, I reckon. A good suet pudding and some meat when you can.'

'I agree, but being cooped up all day in the plait room doesn't help. That's why these afternoons are important.' Jane sighed. Here Jethro was at last, beside her, and yet they talked problems. She wanted to touch him, to have him touch her but it must not be seen by the children. Already Rebecca had noticed something. 'You like him, don't you, Ma,' she had said and Jane had been quick with her reply. 'He's a good friend, Beccy. We need all the friends we can get.'

CHAPTER 11

Arthur Ward stood at Jane's door, a box of produce at his feet. When she opened to him he said cheerfully, 'Hey there, Jane. I heard your little girl had an accident.' The man was wearing a smart jerkin in soft leather over a clean striped shirt.

'Oh, Mr Ward, I don't wish to have you bother with our troubles.'

'Had to come to see if you need help, and I've wanted to have a few words with you.'

She opened the door wider and he picked up the box and carried it inside, placing it among the debris of the family's evening meal. Turning away, he spied Nancy huddled in the cot. 'So you are the girl in the wars. I guess you won't be makin' that mistake twice, hey?'

Nancy nodded and rearranged the thin blanket over her leg.

'Now Jane, you know I offered to help and then you tell me nothing. I had to hear it all from that knuckle-headed son of mine.'

Jane began to reply but he cut her off. 'And I heard about that Roberts fellow being a problem too. He's a cheatin' low life and I've no doubt he's done his best to keep you low too.'

Jane was speechless and stood before him, clasping her hands, her mouth open in surprise. 'Oh, Mr Ward...' she stuttered, wondering exactly what Jethro had told him.

'And that's another thing. You call me Arthur from now on. Let's have less of this Mr Ward nonsense. I guessed you could do with a few provisions so I brought these for you.'

'Oh Mr Ward... Arthur, I can't thank you enough. We're working hard but never seem to earn enough.'

'Good. You come straight to me, agreed? No relying on Jethro. He hasn't the wherewithal to do you much good.'

Jane frowned, but guessing he already knew, she said, 'But he's been a great help to me, Arthur, what with the lifts to town and all.'

'Aye, I heard about that. But don't you go counting on him. He's a dreamer and his heart's not in what he does. I'm your man if you need help.' He paused. 'Although lifts is fine 'cos I'm a busy man, as you know.'

Jane nodded to indicate that she had heard but didn't necessarily agree. Jethro being a dreamer did not tally with what she knew of him. 'The lifts are a life-saver for us and I hope we can keep on with them.'

Arthur Ward made a face and turned away to look around the cottage. 'How much do you pay for this hovel?'

She told him a shilling a week and he glowered, muttering, 'Robbery. I noticed the thatch needs some repair. Does the landlord not come to fix it?'

'I never see him. His agent calls and I keep on at him but nothing gets done. The rain gets in and it's cold. Not good for the children, but we manage.'

'Aye, I expect you do.' He turned to her. 'That son of mine never said a word. Just shows you. He's out a lot these days and I'm guessing he got some little gal somewhere. Not that he would tell me. I'll call on you from time to time if that's all right. Get to know you better since you and me are neighbours. What do you say?'

What could Jane reply but a with a smile and a nod? His help would be welcome but random visits might be a problem.

'Shake on it, Jane,' he said, proffering a hand.

She shook his hand in all gratitude, thanking him for the food, and then showed him out.

The box was full to the top with potatoes, onions, cabbage and a large turnip. There were apples and gooseberries and a joint of mutton with a piece of suet wrapped in a paper. Thanks to Arthur, their immediate problems were solved. They had all this and a few pence in the tin on the shelf. But a thought persisted at the back of Jane's mind. Arthur had warned her off Jethro but it was too late. Her connection with him had become vital to her happiness but it was clear they must be extra careful from now on. She would have to tell him not to dig her garden for if he heard of it, Arthur would react badly. She smiled at his 'little gal' comment, but a dreamer? Jethro was anything but. He talked of bettering himself, just as Dan had done, and farm work had become tedious and exhausting. If he dreamed at all, it was to escape to a better life, just as she herself did.

Coming back from their Sunday trip to the stream, they found Silvie sitting on the step with her girl, Susan.

'There you are, Jane. I've called to see if you'd like my Susan here to call for Stevie in the morning. I reckon we won't be seeing Nancy at school for a bit yet.'

Susan was just a little older than Nancy and they met daily at the plait school.

'Silvie, you are an angel. Stevie would like that, I know.' She pulled him out from behind her skirts. 'I want to start early for the market tomorrow and I'll have to leave Rebecca in charge here. She'll be glad not to have the trip to the school with him and I'll be glad to have her plaiting the whole day. I haven't much to sell this week. Shall I see you at the market?'

'Not till later. I've got my Ivor off with his back and I can't get away early.'

Jane expressed her sorrow at the news. A man who couldn't work must turn to the plaiting to make a few pence and some were not so skilled at it, earning nothing like the eight shillings or so that field work would bring in. 'If it gets bad for you, Silvie, I'll help all I can, though how I can't say at present.'

Silvie smiled her thanks, knowing that most of the women did their best to help each other in the bad times.

Jane left early for Luton the next morning, putting some bread in her pocket by way of breakfast to eat on the way, expecting that Jethro would soon come along to pick her up. She left Stevie waiting for Susan while Nancy and Rebecca made a start on the plaiting.

It was a cold, overcast morning with a heavy dew on the ground and on the verges. Spider webs decked the leafless hedges, heavy with beads of moisture. Jane remembered the carefree days of her childhood when with a soft looped twig she had scooped up the webs until she had collected many layers of gossamer. Jethro soon came along and as usual dropped her close to George Street.

There she sought out her friendly dealer but he did not remember her and paid her only the usual rate for the few scores she offered. There was nothing for it then but to start back for home. She was pushing her way through the arriving crowds when she was hailed by a voice she knew only too well. Roberts sat astride his horse in front of her.

'I just been to your place, Jane Chapman. Them girls told me you'd gone. Done your own sellin' 'ave you? More fool you, eh?'

'I don't have time to waste words with you, Silas Roberts.' Did the man never remember what she had said to him in the past?

'Aw, Jane, don't be unfriendly. I was only there to save you the walk. Seems like I was too late.'

'To take my plait, you mean,' she said.

He slid off the horse and reached for the bridle. 'It's a powerful cold mornin'. I'm on my way to the Lilley Arms in West Street. Hows about you sharin' a flagon of porter with me? It'll warm you up, for it'll be a cold tramp home.'

'No thank you, Silas. I'm quite warm enough without strong drink.' She pulled her shawl more tightly about her shoulders.

'Aw come on, woman. You and me is friends. Come and warm yusself. Have a little fun. I'll throw in a penny meat pie if you fancy. You's my girl after all.'

Jane said nothing and walked past him and on down the road. He called after her. 'Another time, eh? Fix things proper between you and me.'

She ignored his words though the warm drink had been a momentary temptation. Did he really think that pretending a relationship with him made it so? The trouble was, in other circumstances she would have given him a piece of her mind and stopped all the nonsense. Reluctant to be seen shouting in the street, she walked quickly on, passing shops she would never patronise, selling goods she would never be able to afford. She passed the pawnbrokers where she had sold things from the cottage. She paused for a moment to catch her breath outside the clothes shop, its wares were on show, all much worn by many others, most were grimy and threadbare. It was years since she'd had anything new but Nancy needed an underskirt to replace the burned one before she went back to the school. And maybe a better cap than the old torn thing she usually wore.

'Rebecca, have you been crying?'

Rebecca rubbed the dried tears with her free hand. 'Mr Roberts was here, Ma, just after you left. He came into the house but I couldn't stop him. I told him you had gone to the market and he got angry. We were frightened, weren't we, Nancy?'

Nancy was sitting on the side of the cot. 'He did, Ma. I thought he was going to hit us.'

Jane forgot her tiredness and cried, 'What? Tell me exactly what happened.'

'There was this loud knocking on the door and when I opened it he was standing there wearing a frock coat I'd never seen before,' started Rebecca. 'He said, *Where's your Ma? I've come for her plait.* I didn't want to say you had walked to the market 'cos I don't trust him. He said, *What's the matter with you? You knows I buy her plait.* I told him you don't want to sell to him and he wasn't coming to the house no more. He pushed me aside and came in. *Who said that? Weren't me,* he said. *I give as good a price as anyone.* He was looking around at everything. Then he bent down and pushed his horrible face close to mine. *So she thinks she can go it alone, does she? Well, we'll soon see about that.* Then he turned and went out.'

Rebecca was clasping and unclasping her hands, her face anxious. 'I was panicking, Ma. What if he lay in wait for you along the road? I wanted to run out and catch you but Nancy said no. She said to stay here. That's what you'd want, she said.'

'She's right, Beccy. You are safe here. I can cope with Mr Roberts, don't you fear.'

125

Towards evening, Jane heard her name called from the garden and from the window she saw Jessie standing on the path, her feet apart, her arms akimbo and an annoyed look on her face. Jane went to her door. 'What is it, Jessie?'

'What happened to that deal we had. You forgot about that, did you?'

At once Jane realised she had forgotten to tell Silvie that Susy had to call for Jessie's two. 'You heard about Nancy's accident? It was such a to-do that it clean drove it from my mind.'

The woman gave a loud snort. 'All I know is no one calls for my two. One of my girls has to do it and loses an hour's plaitin'. That's how much I can depend on you.'

An hour? It was fifteen minutes to the school and ten minutes for the girl to walk back. 'I'm sorry, Jessie, but you can surely understand…'

Jessie cut in. 'I'm not payin' you for a no-show.'

'Alright, I've said I'm sorry. Nancy can't walk and I was hard put to it to cope. I accepted help from a friend.'

'That's as maybe, but a deal's a deal.'

'Nancy'll do it when she can walk. Meanwhile…'

'Oh yes, and when will that be?'

'She's making progress.'

Jessie made a dismissive gesture and folded her arms. 'Them'll be old enough to go by thesselves by then. I want no deal. I 'ave to pay that money to my own girls.'

Jane wondered why this had not been possible in the first place. Surely what they all earned from plaiting covered the pence Jessie might have paid to Jane. She watched the woman turn and stalk away, leaving her half glad and half ashamed. She didn't like falling short on her commitments and, of course, it would have an effect on her budget.

CHAPTER 12

When Susan brought Stevie home Jane asked him if he'd mentioned that they should call for Joey and Dody.

'No Ma, I forgot. I like walking with Susan. She told me to call her Suzy. Have I got to go with Joey?'

'No dear, not any more. Soon you'll be old enough to go on your own.'

'I can do it now, Ma.'

'When you reach five, Stevie, then you can. And it's your birthday soon, isn't it, so you won't have long to wait.'

At dusk, Jethro came, carrying his spade. Jane had just put Stevie in the 'big bed' that thrilled him so much and the sight of Jethro at her door swept her mind clear of trouble and doubt.

When Jane and Dan had married, she had inherited her parent's iron bedstead. The couple had bought a straw-filled mattress and a long bolster. Somehow along the way they had acquired some second-hand sheets and blankets and a chamber pot for under the bed, that they had laughingly called the gazunder. Now Jane tucked Stevie in where usually she slept alone. Before Nancy's accident, both girls had shared another straw mattress on the floor.

For the next few days Jane walked around in a joyful cloud. Nancy's wound was healing well, the fine was paid, and because of the happy atmosphere, their fingers worked swiftly over the straw and the coils for sale grew satisfactorily. Suzy still called for Stevie and brought him back at the end of the day.

Every evening, Jane sat in the candlelight, trembling with anticipation but often Jethro did not come. During the day she walked around the cottage to the garden. The sight of the black clumps of dug earth consoled her. It had not been a dream after all and she knew he would call when he could.

On the Sunday, she took the children to the woods as usual. They went slowly because still Nancy could only limp. When they came to the farm, Arthur hailed them from the gate.

'I guessed you'd be coming by.' He nodded to the bunch of splints under her arm and the trailing length of plait. 'Still at it, I see.'

'Needs must, Mr Ward, I mean, Arthur. This week we have done well.' They chatted for a while then Jane turned to go, hearing him call out, 'Wait, Jane, what say you and me get together on a regular basis.'

She was standing some yards away from him and chose to misunderstand his words. 'You'd be welcome to visit any time, Arthur.' Then before she saw his face to fall, she went on her way.

The next time Jethro came to the cottage, he brought a bucket of horse manure. Jane smiled when she saw it. 'Oh, what a lovely gift you have brought me.'

'I'll bring a bit at a time and dig it into what I've turned over. You'll see the benefit in the spring.'

There was no need now for the shy, tentative hinting about how they felt for each other.

'I take it you've been kept busy these past few days.'

He nodded. 'Er, yes, we've got the castrating going on and the corn sales but Da keeps his eye on me. This evening he's gone to the town. He saw an advertisement in the newspaper for some exercise club.'

'Surely he doesn't need that. You'd think he did more than enough exercise.'

'He took off yesterday and came back with his beard and his hair cut. I nearly laughed but that wouldn't do. He'd clap me in irons if he saw me laugh.'

Jethro went off to dig some more of the garden, leaving a thoughtful Jane to consider his words. She knew what was in Arthur's mind and she guessed Jethro did too. After his comment on Sunday, Arthur had made his wishes explicit. He had followed her with his eyes from the farm gate and it left her with a problem. He was not exactly rich, but was not unattractive and not so old, single and, if Jethro was correct, in need of a good woman. What would he do when he discovered her affections lay in the direction of his son? Thinking on it made her shiver. He was a powerful man and could make life awful for Jethro and for her too if he did not have his way. He must never, never find out.

But how was she to respond to his kindness and at the same time reject any further overtures he might make? The possible complications of the situation possessed her for some time until a good hour later she heard the clink of a bucket on the step, and opening the door, she pulled Jethro inside. She put her arms around him and whispered into his ear. 'Nancy is fast off but we must be very quiet. Yesterday she told me she'd had a dream where she was looking over this room and saw her Da sitting at the table with me. I asked her what we were doing and she said just talking and she couldn't remember more.'

'What did you tell her?' he whispered back.

'I told her it was just a wishful thought her mind had conjured and that's what dreams were.'

'Did she accept that?'

'I think so. She's only a child, after all.' She had been whispering these words into his ear but now she kissed it. He turned his head and caught her lips in his. They were pressed close and she felt the hardness of him and wished with all her heart that they were alone. She closed her eyes and held herself steady, fearing her knees would give way. Her heart was thumping. 'Can you feel it?' she asked her voice trembling.

He took her hand and pressed it to his own chest. 'I can.' His own heart was racing too.

'Come to the table,' she murmured, needing to sit until she felt calmer.

Jane made tea and in low voices they talked until Nancy stirred, when they fell silent. Jane looked over at her restless child. 'As soon as she can climb the steps, she'll go above to sleep.'

'But the boy?'

'It will be difficult to prise him from my bed.'

Jethro nodded, understanding at once.

When it was time to go, she went outside with him. It was a bright, starlit night, clear and cold. It was quiet except for loud voices in the distance. The dim candlelight from Jessie's cottage was just discernible among the trees. Some squabble was taking place with different voices coming over the still air. Jethro hugged her tightly then turned to go. The smell from the bucket reminded her. 'Don't forget your bucket,' she murmured, picking it up and handing it to him.

The next day, Jessie stood at the end of the path to the cottage. 'Has your man come back from the dead?'

Jane bent to throw her bowl of soapy water over the flowers. 'What do you mean?'

'Couldn't see well last night when I comes out but I saw a shadow of a man in your garden. Heard the clink of a shovel on stone, I did. Someone there? Looks like someone's been diggin'. Don't see you out there with a spade.'

Jane's heart gave a jolt. 'You don't know what we do over here, Jessie, and I think you must have been mistaken about a man. Are you sure you weren't sleep walking?'

Jessie huffed and frowned. 'Not likely. We was havin' a blarney 'cos my Maisie is expecting, stupid girl. Just about to start in service but now Flo must go in her stead. I comes out 'cos her screechin' was doin' my ears no good.'

'Maisie pregnant? You aren't too happy about that, I suppose.'

'Ah, ain't no matter. What's wrong with one more, I say, but our Flo is ravin' mad about it. She don't want to go cleanin' out other folks chamber pots or washin' floors and all that. She's a lazy cow.'

Jane wasn't surprised by the news but wondered which of the local boys was the father. 'No chance of a wedding?'

'Nah, that bleedin' lodger's outstayed his welcome.' Jessie looked towards the back of the cottage, wrinkling her nose. 'That privy of yours is a bit ripe when the wind blows our way. You gonna do summat about that?'

'I'll tip some earth in it when I get the time,' Jane replied., thinking that here was another source of anxiety. Was Jessie sure she had seen someone and if so, did she recognise who it was? Jessie was a nosey woman. It was hard enough keeping a secret in the village but Jessie was a particular threat. Not only was she nosey but she was a gossip too. If she ever recognised Jethro the story would soon be all over the village and before long straight to Arthur Ward's ears. Her heart sank at the thought. She must warn Jethro; ask him to stay away. How could she bear not to have that small time they had together? I'll just tell him to stop digging, she told herself, yet spent the rest of the day worrying about it.

CHAPTER 13

Two days later, it was Stevie's birthday and Jane prepared a special tea for when he came home from the plait school. She made oatcakes with jam and half a boiled egg each and apples on sticks covered in burnt sugar toffee. Afterwards she gave him the little bag of raspberry drops she had hidden until this moment. To Nancy and Rebecca she gave a barley stick each so they wouldn't feel left out.

Stevie was happy. 'Can I give one to Dody, Ma?'

'Of course, if you wish.'

Nancy said, 'But don't give any to Joey.'

'No, I won't,' he declared. 'I'm five now. I can go to school on my own, can't I, Ma? You said I could.'

'Do you really want to?'

'Course I do. I like Suzy but she's a girl and she only talks to all the big girls.' His tone was one of disgust at this offence to his male pride.

'Well, I'll tell her not to come any more then.'

'Okay.' He popped a raspberry drop into his mouth and sat sucking happily.

The next morning Jane explained to Suzy that she needn't call for Stevie any longer. While he hunted for his cap, she said to the girl, 'You are a sensible girl, Suzy, you don't have to walk with him but just keep an eye from a distance.'

'In case he gets lost?'

'No dear, he won't get lost, but it's the other boys I worry about. He's small for his age and not as strong as he thinks he is.'

'Alright,' Suzy said, 'I'll stay close by.'

'And here is tuppence for you for helping me all this time. Tell your Ma that any time she needs help she can call on me.'

'Yes, thanks, Mrs Chapman,' and the girl skipped off home.

At the end of the day, Jane was eagerly looking out for Stevie. Even from a distance she could tell all was not well. He was limping and his face looked swollen.

Her heart sinking, she called, 'What happened to you?'

Stevie stumbled up the path, on the verge of tears. 'I had a fight with Joey 'cos he took my sweets.'

'Was this going to school or coming home?'

'Coming home. I gave Dody one at break time and he saw. He knowed I had them in my pocket and he wanted them. I wouldn't give them to him so he pushed me in a bush and grabbed the bag. I hit him, Ma, I did, but he hit me back and then we had a fight, but it weren't no good. The other boys were yelling for him to kick me so he did.'

'Is that why you are limping? He is a bully, and I'll have a word with his Ma.'

'No Ma, you mustn't. He'll only set on me again. I'll fight him again if I have to.'

'You have to be really bricky to stand up to bullies, Stevie.'

'I know, but he's bigger than me. I'm gonna lose every time. And I ain't got no sweets now 'cos he took them all.'

'Well, my little chuckaboo, it just so happens I kept some back when I saw you were taking them to school, perhaps to share them out. You can have them after your tea.'

Jane's inclination at first was to recall Suzy but soon realised this would not help matters. Stevie would be called a namby-pamby and lose face. He must learn to stand up for himself. It would be hard but she mustn't pamper him if he were to grow stronger. She should not interfere in his battles, no mother should, so tomorrow he would have to find his way to school and back as best he could.

The next day Stevie had bruises but would not tell her about them. Each day there was something, and over time she noticed his growing reluctance to go to the school. Often Jane asked him how things were going but he would never say. She would insist, 'Is he still punching you?'

'No Ma, not any more.'

That was a relief but why then was Stevie so quiet and miserable? 'Do you see him when you go in the morning?'

'Sometimes.'

'Does he call you names?'

'No, Ma.' Stevie turned away and refused to answer more questions, leaving Jane frowning and anxious.

So it was a mystery to Jane why her cheerful son had become this morose, unhappy child, who looked thinner than before. Sometimes she made an excuse and walked to the school with him. Sometimes they came upon Joey. 'Mornin' Mrs Chapman,' he would say and then 'Mornin' Stevie.' and go on his way.

'He seems friendly enough,' she remarked to Stevie.

'Yes,' said her glum little boy.

It was several weeks later when she noticed he was walking in a stilted fashion. 'Do your legs hurt?' she asked him. 'Has he been kicking you?'

'No, Ma.'

Jane and the girls were mostly busy with the plaiting and weeks went by before she realised he was lowering himself gently into a chair as a pained expression flitted over his face.

'Does your bottom hurt, Stevie. Have you hurt yourself there?'

Always it was the same answer. 'No, Ma.'

Nancy could now climb the ladder to her bed with Rebecca, and Stevie was still sleeping in the big bed with Jane. When Jethro called in the evenings, the downstairs room was free of children and at last they could be alone. He had heeded her warnings about Jessie, made sure no one was about as he finished the garden and the neat area lay in waiting for the spring sowing.

Jane had only the smallest hand mirror in which to check her hair but her hands were all too obviously worn, with reddened skin and callouses and ingrained dirt. She did what she could to smarten herself up. She soaked her hands and removed the grime left by heavy work. She trimmed her nails and worked grease into the palms and fingers to make them as soft as she could. She washed her hair then combed and brushed it until the curls were shiny and luxurious. She put on her Sunday best skirt and a muslin blouse she had made in the quiet of the evenings. When the children had gone to bed she touched her throat and ears with a little bergamot and sat prepared, knowing what was sure to happen.

When Jethro came they lay together on the day bed. He was vigorous but she was experienced so their coupling was a revelation to them both. Her woman's body, so soft and so responsive to his touch, bewitched him. She guided him, showed him, taught him until they were tuned to each other's needs. Sometimes it was raw passion, sometimes a symphony of sweetness and love.

143

Curled together in that tiny space, he whispered often, 'Sweet, wonderful Jane.'

'Say it again,' she would say.

And with a kiss, he would repeat, 'Sweetest and most wonderful Jane.'

It was balm to her starved heart. 'Again,' and she would nuzzle his neck and kiss his throat.

Afterwards, when they were up and dressed, she told him of her worries about Stevie.

'He's changed, he's not the same boy and I swear he's getting thinner though I do my best to feed him well. I am afraid he will disappear completely. He walks cautiously and I think it hurts him to sit. But most of all is his silence. He won't talk to me like he used to. I ask what is troubling him but he won't say.'

Jethro frowned and thought for a long moment. 'Tell me, who does he spend time with when he's not at home?'

'He's at the plait school all day; why do you ask?'

'I have heard the men talking so I know a little of the ways of some men.'

'He never talks to any men.'

'Can you be sure? Have you asked the mistress if Stevie is always there or does he play hooky?'

'I can't believe he would. He's too young to even know of it and someone would tell me if he was not there.'

'Led by older boys perhaps?'

'I don't know,' she cried despairingly. 'He often has bruises.'

'Does he let you wash him?'

'Not now. He declares he's too old to have his mother wash him.'

'This is worrying. You need to look him all over.'

Jane looked at him, her eyes wide. 'What am I looking for?'

'Maybe nothing. Just look.' His off-hand tone puzzled Jane so when Jethro had gone Jane prepared herself for bed. She took a candle up the ladder and found all the children fast asleep. Turning to her own bed she gently pulled back the blanket over Stevie, careful not to drip hot wax on the sleeping boy.

He was lying on his side, his nightshirt rucked up around his hips. She lowered the candle and examined him. There were some marks, perhaps old bruises. She could not tell in the candlelight what these marks were. She covered him and decided to look in the morning.

Jane did not sleep well for worrying about what Jethro had said, so was up and dressed early the next morning. When she returned from the privy she found Stevie sitting at the table.

'I don't want to go to school today, Ma,' he said

'Why, Stevie, do you feel ill? Have you a stomach ache?'

'No, I just don't want to.'

Hoping to provoke an explanation from him, she said, 'But if you're not ill, you have to, unless you give me a good reason.'

146

He didn't reply but just sat looking glum. Jane climbed the steps to rouse the girls and fetch down the chamber pot for emptying. She examined his nightshirt and saw stains. They looked like blood. Had he cut himself? Sat on something sharp? Perhaps been pushed over and fallen backwards onto a sharp stone? She stood for a moment trying to imagine what might have happened, puzzling why Stevie should want to keep the hurt from her. Then she quickly rolled the garment into a ball, bent to pick up the chamber pot and went down.

When she got there he was gone. Perhaps he was hiding, but of course in the cottage there was nowhere to hide. She went outside the door and called his name. After a moment, when there was no reply she went indoors and took her shawl and wrapped it tightly around her. Rebecca and Nancy were down and at the table. Rebecca said 'Where's Stevie? Has he gone to school already? I know he likes to be early.'

'I'm going to look for him. Give Nancy some breakfast. I'll be back soon.'

She looked in the privy and up and down the lane but there was no sign of him. She picked her way through the long grass behind the privy but did not believe he could have gone there. The frost on the grass was undisturbed. She stood for a moment wondering where he could have gone and then thought of Ward's Wood, the only other likely place.

She started up the track, and nearing the farm she met a farmworker making for the yard. 'Have you seen my boy?' she called. He turned and pointed further up towards the trees.

Jane started to run. When she reached the place where they usually sat to picnic she saw him. He sat hunched over his knees, his head low and resting on his arms. She approached slowly and sat down beside him on the wet grass. 'There you are, Stevie. You had me worried.'

He lifted his head and looked at her sadly. 'Sorry, Ma.'

'It doesn't matter if you don't want to go. You can stay with us today. But I want to know what is troubling you. Maybe if you tell me, I can help. It isn't like you to be so miserable and I miss my cheerful boy.'

He looked away, his lip trembling, his fingers clutching the sleeves of his jacket, still unable to speak.

'Can you not tell me, Stevie? We can put it right together. Is it something at school?'

He shook his head.

'On the road then? On the way there and back?'

Again he shook his head.

'Is it someone then?' He did not shake his head. 'Someone I know?' Slowly, he nodded.

She paused, thinking of any possible people, then thought of Joey, bully boy Joey, of course. 'Is Joey bullying you?'

With obvious reluctance, Stevie replied. 'Sort of.'

Jane looked away over the stream running near their feet. 'Does Joey hurt you?'

He nodded dumbly. She thought of the stains on his nightshirt. 'How does he hurt you?'

Stevie's lip was trembling. At first she thought he wasn't going to answer, then he muttered, 'Lots of ways,' then he clamped his lips shut. Trying to keep her voice as level as she could, she said, 'But where does he do this?'

'Behind the school at dinner time. It hurts, Ma.'

Jane was silent. Stevie was no doubt reluctant to tell on Joey for fear of worse persecution. That monster Joey was only one year older than her boy. The thought of all those months of torture without disclosing a word made her frown. 'What exactly does he do?

Again there was a silence, then he said, 'Rude things.'

This time Jane was lost for words. What rude things? Her imagination faltered but she was not surprised when Stevie refused to say more. He was probably too embarrassed to go into details, or was it shame he was feeling?

Jane was frozen where she sat, blind to the scene around her, concentrating hard on what her son had told her, on his pain and confusion. A terrible sense of horror was making her tremble and there was a prickling in her neck and down her back. What were these rude things that Jethro had hinted at? She could not imagine what a small child might do to another but whatever it was, it was appalling. Taking a moment to regain control of her imagination, she gathered Stevie to her and held him close. It was a while before she could speak with determination. 'I don't need you to tell me any more, Stevie, but this has to stop. I shall see to that. He won't hurt you any more, believe me. It is a good thing you told me.'

'I was afraid to tell you, Ma. I was shamed. He said if I told anyone he would knock my head off.'

'You have nothing to be ashamed of, Stevie. It is that Joey who should be ashamed.'

'You won't tell anyone, will you?'

'I can see you don't want me to but I can't ignore this. He's a wicked boy and he must be stopped. But don't worry, I'll think about what must be done without making things worse for you. Let's go home now.'

They both got up and made their way slowly down the track, Jane wondering what she was going to say to Jessie. When they reached the cottage, Jane cast a warning look at her curious daughters, stilling their questions. 'Stevie will be home with us for a while, girls. We'll give him some jobs to keep him busy and that will leave more time for the plaiting.' She looked sharply from one to the other, assuming their agreement.

Later in the day, when an atmosphere of normality had returned to the room, Jane told them she wanted to borrow some washing soap from their neighbour. Suspecting nothing, they continued their work happily as Jane made her way to Jessie's cottage. She was still seething with fury but hid it as best she could. 'Come out, Jessie, I need to talk to you,' she yelled when she reached the cottage.

Jessie opened the door. 'What is it now?'

'It's your Joey. He's been bullying my Stevie. He tells me he hurts him and does nasty things I can't repeat.'

'What you fussing about? Where's the harm in that? Scrapping is normal for all boys. Your boy has to learn to fight back.'

'Oh, it is not just fighting but God knows what else, crude disgusting things. He's been bullying my boy for weeks.'

Jessie burst out laughing. 'Is that all? What's so terrible about that? Leave 'em alone to grow up natural, that's what I always say.'

'Is that so? Left to their own devices they turn into nasty, filthy-minded little tykes like your Joey. Is that your idea of good parenting?'

'Oooh,' hooted Jessie. 'You is so respec'able, ain't you? Good parenting, eh, what book reading 'ave you been doin'? I knows more about bringin' up kids than you'll ever know, what with all my experience.'

'Look, let me warn you, Jessie, if your Joey lays one more finger on my boy I'll be straight down to the police station and have him up before the constables. That would ruin your reputation as a parent, wouldn't it?'

Jessie laughed again. 'Let's see how far you get with that, Mrs High and Mighty.'

Having delivered her warning, Jane turned to go just as Joey and Dody came home. Jane strode up to the boy, who looked suddenly fearful in that moment as she took hold of his ear. He squirmed in her grip but she held on.

'Right now, you listen to me, you dirty-minded little devil. You touch Stevie one more time with a finger, a hand or a sharp stone and I'll have the constable on to you as quick as I can get him.'

'We was just playin' around, Missis.'

'I don't know what sort of game you call that but I won't have it, do you hear me?'

The boy broke free and ran to his mother, who called, 'You leave my boy alone, Jane Chapman! If anyone is to punish him, it will be me.'

Jane thought this so unlikely that she stalked away without another word. Her anger was only partly mollified but she could do no more except hope her words had been sufficiently strong to have an effect.

She knew now that any neighbourly relations with any of Jessie's family were at an end. This was no great hardship but of them all, she feared for Dody, who already had a cowed, put-upon look about her. How could that little girl cope in a household where unmarried girls brought forth fatherless babies and neglect was routine?

CHAPTER 14

It was a good move to keep Stevie at home. Gradually she saw hints emerge of the lively child she knew. There were many jobs he could do that freed Jane up to do more plaiting. The first job she gave him was to cut an old newspaper into squares for the privy and thread a length of string through the corners. He could clear the ashes from the grate; he could scrub and scrape vegetables after a fashion and sweep up the cut straws from the floor. After the dirty clothes were soaked overnight, he could help with the dolly and hanging the clothes to dry.

One Saturday afternoon in December, Arthur Ward called. He wore a smart waistcoat and his hair and beard had been trimmed, a silk kerchief was knotted around his neck and his boots were clean and shiny. To hide her surprise, she hurried to ask him in.

The children were sitting around the table. Rebecca was teaching Stevie his letters, making him draw them out with his finger in the tray she had made for the purpose. It had a layer of sand taken from the lane and if Stevie did not shape his Bs and his Gs to her satisfaction, she shook the tray, removing his attempts so that he could try again. Nancy was practising her plaiting of the more elaborate Brilliant style, a skill that needed much practise while she listened to the lesson.

Arthur said, 'I won't come in, Jane, but I would ask you to walk with me for a while.'

Puzzled yet curious, Jane reached for her shawl and closed the door behind her and together they walked to the lane.

'Let us go this way. I know whose cottage is over there.'

'Oh yes, my neighbour.'

'I know of her. A real church bell. You can hear her all over the village.'

Jane mumbled her agreement but was reluctant to talk about Jessie. 'This way goes to nowhere,' she said.

'The lane abuts one of my fields.' Arthur paused and surveyed the tall yellowing stalks. 'I tried American corn this year but it didn't do well.'

'I wondered what it was. Has the farm done well in general this year?'

'Quite well, Jane. We'll be having a good Christmas this year.'

Jane did not comment. The festival was almost upon them and she was hoping to have at least one festive meal as a treat for the children. She had read in the newspaper that families in London decorated a small fir tree but she didn't know with what. Nobody in the village could afford such fripperies. The most villagers would do was collect holly, ivy and mistletoe to decorate their rooms, and have a good meal on the day with a great deal of beer and porter.

'Oh yes,' Arthur went on. 'We'll manage a fowl and a plum pudding, no doubt.'

Jane had planned to give the children an especially rich clanger, a local suet pudding usually given to men in the locality to eat at lunchtime. It was a roll of dough with meat or bacon at one end and fruit or jam at the other. She was saving dried fruit and would add as much meat as she could afford when the time came. That was the nearest she could get to a 'fowl'.

'But that is not what I wanted to discuss with you, Jane. I have noticed how hard you work, and how good you are with your children. I have a mind to fill the gap left by my dead wife and my thinking fell on you. I can give you a more comfortable life than what you have at this moment. If you are willing to consider what I am offering, then I propose we get to know each other better.'

The words came out in a rush as if much rehearsed and she listened open-mouthed. This was more than just a fancy that she could ignore. How could she reply? It was a generous offer that any woman in her situation would rate as fortunate, if, as she supposed, he was offering marriage. A wealthy man prepared to take on a widow with three children was a rarity. In her present straitened state it was indeed a stroke of luck she would be mad to reject.

Jane took a deep breath. 'Arthur, you have overwhelmed me again. I cannot give you any sort of answer for it is too big a surprise.'

'I realise that. I want you to think hard and make sure it is what you would want. I fear I have shocked you but I could think of no other way once the plan had formed in my mind.'

'But we know very little of each other.'

'Exactly. That is why we must spend time together. And then when you are sure and you have some feelings for me, you can give me an answer.'

Jane paused in the slow steps she had been taking as he spoke. Yes, that was where the difficulty lay. She had loved Daniel with all her heart otherwise she would not have given up her old life to be with him. Now she loved Jethro with much the same fervour. Arthur was pleasant but she knew she would never have feelings for him. Added to that, he had given no hint of having feelings for her. Perhaps he just wanted practical help round the farm and in the house, or maybe, as Jethro said, he was just lonely. With her expression as sincere as she could make it, she said, 'Arthur I am much honoured by your plan but I must think about this.'

'But you are not greatly opposed to the idea?'

'I don't know, Arthur. I really don't know what I feel.'

'Then I will leave you to mull over what I am proposing.'

'Thank you, Arthur, I shall do that.'

They both turned on the spot and made their way back to the cottage. As they neared it, Arthur looked over it and commented on the damaged thatch. 'Do you have the rain get in?'

'I do but I have bowls and buckets under the drips. I have to admit that the thatch barely has time to dry out.'

'So who is your landlord?'

'It is his agent who comes for the rent. The landlord I never see. I tell the man what needs repairing but nothing is ever done.'

'But yours is not as bad as the others here.'

'Dan did a lot to improve it, but now, of course…' She did not go on, fearing it would sound as if she were pleading for help and that she would not do. She stopped at her garden path and Arthur continued up the track to his farm. Then he turned and called back to her and called out, 'We killed a pig yesterday. I'll send down some pork.'

Jane put both hands on her breast to indicate her gratitude, nodded and smiled. Then she went indoors.

'What did he want, Ma?' Nancy asked.

'Never you mind. That is my business,' Jane replied.

For the rest of the day Jane was seriously worried about this new situation. Arthur would expect an answer and before that, who could guess what he might expect them to do together? Her only comfort lay in her children who were too young to be left without her, neither by day or by night. And then what would Jethro say when she told him, as she must. It was clear in her own mind what she wanted to do. Arthur must be refused, but how was she to do it in the least disastrous way? If she were ever to tell Arthur that she had her own plans involving his son, the revelation would be explosive and who could foretell what he would do then? It surely would not be anything good.

The problem was such a vexation just when she was looking forward to a calm few weeks after all the recent drama. The court case, the fine, Nancy's accident and Stevie's trouble all had taken their toll on her peace of mind. In a week or two would come Christmas with no hope of a worry-free and joyous time.

For over two years she had been alone and willingly so. Now there were two men, one a deep and loving comfort to her and one an unwelcome intruder on her happiness. How could this mix of good and bad be counted as good fortune?

Jane was in two minds about going to the wood the next day. The likelihood of meeting Arthur Ward as they passed the farm was high and it would be embarrassing to have him hail her after their talk. However, she badly wanted to see Jethro and if they went, perhaps he would join them. If he did not she would have to wait until Monday morning and tell him on the way to the market.

As it happened the weather turned bad and after church they had to stay home The downpour kept them busy emptying the bowls and basins catching the leaks in the bedroom. Stevie did his best to light a fire because it was so cold and it was only late in the afternoon that the rain gave way to a weak sun.

'Put on all the warm clothes you have,' Jane told the children. 'We'll go and cut some holly for the house. No need to go to the wood, we'll go along the lane and search the hedgerows.'

Chasing up and down the lane soon warmed everyone. They went past the sorry crop of corn that Arthur had talked of and Jane was able to tell the children about it. There were no cottages past their own and the lane soon narrowed into an overgrown old drovers' lane, muddy and unused. Soon they had armfuls of ivy and holly sprigs with lots of berries, so to avoid the muddiest puddles, they turned for home.

'When is Christmas, Ma?' Stevie asked and Rebecca answered, 'It's next week. Shall we put all this up now or shall we wait a few days?'

'We'll leave it in the garden for a bit. It'll come to no harm,' Jane said.

Once indoors the girls' cheeks were rosy with every appearance of good health after the walk but Stevie looked tired and pale with no such glow. Jane made him sit by the embers of the fire and added more gorse and twigs to make a blaze. He shivered, so she took the blanket from the day bed and wrapped it around him, then rubbed his hands and arms vigorously, murmuring, 'I do hope going out has not given you a chill, Stevie.' Then she put the cooking pot over the fire, added some water, two onions, two carrots and some chopped turnips. 'We'll have some soup for supper to go with those cold potatoes.'

The dark descended swiftly in the evenings now and to save on candles, they all went to bed early. The bedroom was cold and damp and the girls cuddled together for warmth, adding shawls and extra clothes on top of them. Jane let Stevie sleep in his clothes just this once and took the daybed blanket upstairs to give him extra warmth. When she joined him in the big bed, she pulled him close to the heat of her own body, hoping that his chill would be gone in the morning.

When they woke they discovered a light sprinkling of snow on everything outside. Jane rose first to build a fire and only when she thought the room warm enough did she call the others to come down.

Glad that she did not have to walk to the market, she stacked their scores of plait close to the door, ready to go. Then she mixed oatmeal and a little fat with water and salt, and fried the cakes in her skillet for their breakfast.

She felt Stevie's forehead when he came down but he was not feverish. 'Stay in the warm today, love, just in case,' she told him.

The man standing at the door later that morning, said, 'I've come to do your roof, Missis,'

'Really? Who sent you?' she asked. His face was vaguely familiar to her.

'That Mr Ward from up the farm.' He tilted his head in the direction of the track. 'I'm the thatcher an' he says to mend yer damage.'

'Alright, but I can't pay you,' Jane said, afraid there would be a bill she could not afford.

'No need, Missis, Mr Ward will cover it.'

Jane was so glad to have the roof repaired but she realised that now she was more than ever in Arthur's debt, what with this, the vegetables, and the pork he'd promised. All these made it more difficult for her to refuse him. Of course, it was easy for him to do these kindnesses, but nevertheless it was thoughtful and generous and made her feel kindly towards him, which was perhaps what he intended.

As she worked, she could hear the man as he carted the bunches of reeds up his ladder, placed them in position then pegged them down, first the under layer and then a top layer. Stevie wanted to go out and watch and she let him. He swore he was not cold and ran in to tell her he had helped by fetching the leggett that the man had dropped.

'What is a leggett?' the girls wanted to know.

'It's his tool for tapping the straws to make them tidy,' said Stevie proudly. 'I'm going to be a thatcher when I grow up.'

But Jane was obsessed with her own thoughts until finally, she gave up. Arthur could do what he liked but she would take a long time to give him an answer and just see how things went. If he pressed more charity on her, she would think of an excuse and refuse it. He would soon find out that she would not be manipulated.

Soon after the thatcher started his work, Mr Roberts arrived. 'Howz my best girl today?' he said when she opened the door. He was wearing a new hat and to her mind he looked ridiculous. 'What's that on your head?'

'Latest thing this. Called a bowler. Smart, don'tcha think?' He grinned and winked. 'Got to keep up with the fashion these days.'

'I told you not to call. I'll not deal with you. Don't you ever listen to what I say?'

'You women allus say the opposite of what yer mean. No means yes in my book. Never take a woman serious, that's my policy. Come on now, admit it. You needs me to take your plait.' He looked up to where he heard tapping on the roof. 'Who you got up there?' His jocular mood had deserted him. 'How long is he goin' to be around? He better watch hisself or I'll be on to 'im.'

'What's it to you?' Jane tried to close the door but his foot was in the way.

'I was just wonderin' how your kids were doin'. Goin' back to school yet, are they?'

Jane frowned at the rapid change of tack.

'Got to learn their plaitin', ain't they? Learn all they can 'cos that means more money for you. I'd send 'em back toot sweet if it were me.'

Jane aimed a kick at the ankle of the foot in the door. 'Go away, I'm busy!' she shouted as he grunted.

There was plenty to do. In the evenings when the children were in bed she knitted and sewed and wrapped sweets to fill the children's stockings on Christmas morning.

Jethro came as often as he could. His father was out more regularly in the evenings, for as a landowner he had social obligations at this time. He went to meetings, to the tavern and played in local games, tournaments, all activities more frequent in the festive season. Jane came to rely on her lover's more frequent visits as they grew closer, each enraptured with the charms of the other. At night, they lay together on the narrow daybed, locked in each other's arms. Then came the time when she told him of his father's proposal.

'I knew something was up. He said something odd the other day, just out of the blue, asked me how I would fancy another mother. I told him one mother was enough and I didn't need no other, but I fear he's serious, Jane.'

Jane giggled. 'Would you like me as your mother?'

His face clouded. 'Don't joke about this. What are you going to tell him?'

She kissed him. 'Nothing. I'll drag it out until he gets fed up and forgets the idea.'

He grunted. 'You don't know my father when he wants something, Jane. If he ever finds out about us… well, I hate to think what he would do. He's a hard man underneath all that cheerful show.'

'Then we must be careful and not run any risks. You know I love only you, Jethro.'

CHAPTER 15

Every year, at Christmas time, the vicar of St Peter's arranged a feast for all the children of Lilley. It was held in the church hall on Boxing Day and was paid for by the wealthy landowners in the area as most of the older boys worked for them throughout the year. Rebecca and Nancy had attended the previous year and they were looking forward to the event. Stevie would be allowed to go this year.

After the tea, there would be games and prizes and at the end of the afternoon the children would be sent home with something good to eat, like fruit or bonbons or barley sugar sticks. This was exciting enough to look forward to, but there was Christmas Eve and Christmas Day to enjoy first.

On Christmas Eve, the excited children pinned up their stockings on the shelf beside the fire and when the cottage was quiet of their merry chatter, Jane filled them with all she had prepared. There was an apple in the toe of each, then lots of sweets and finally a gift she had made for each, wrapped in white paper with a red ribbon. Nancy had a peg doll, fully dressed in clothes Jane had sewn. Rebecca had ribbons and a pretty clip for her hair and Stevie had a bag of marbles. There were also scarves and woolly hats she had knitted for each of them.

For the dinner, Jethro had brought her a rabbit so there was no need for a true Bedfordshire clanger after all. She stewed the rabbit with potatoes, herbs and vegetables and made a suet pudding filled with a handful of currants which they would have with some treacle.

On Christmas morning, Rebecca shyly gave her mother a pincushion she had made, stuffed with lavender from their garden. She had helped Stevie to make a Christmas card with *Happy Christmas Ma* in erratic lettering, the best he could manage. Nancy gave Jane a package containing a comb and had sewn a handkerchief with *Jane* in chain stitch in the corner.

'I bought the comb with my own money, Ma,' she said proudly.

The room was filled with the greenery they had collected and rang with laughter as they played games together. Only Jane had a small sadness in her, for only Jethro's presence would complete her happiness. His cousin Thomas and his wife were visiting from Dunstable so he could not leave his family to visit her on Christmas Day.

They all went to bed warm and happy and the next morning put on their best clothes in readiness for the afternoon's event. Rebecca, with some of her new ribbons tied in her hair, walked with them to the church hall. Jessie's three youngest walked there too, everyone being on their best behaviour lest denied entrance to the hall.

Back in the cottage, Jane swept the floor and cleared the grate, then tidied as much as she could before sitting in the big chair to rest, grateful for a little time alone to daydream. For a while she dozed in the chair but was woken by Rebecca stamping the snow off her shoes as she came in.

'Why, Beccy, what time is it? Where are the others?'

'I left early, Ma. I was worried. I left them playing the games.'

'But you had the tea? Why were you worried?'

'I saw Silas Roberts go by in his cart from the hall window. I could tell by that daft hat he wears. I was afraid he was on his way to you.'

'Oh, you sweet girl. He hasn't been anywhere near me. Were you afraid he might do me harm?'

'He knows we were all at the tea. I thought he might want to catch you on your own like last time.' Rebecca looked shamefaced.

'Well, I'm hoping he's learned his lesson, Beccy. But you mustn't spend your time worrying about me, you know. I would kick him again where it hurts most if he ever tried that again, dear.' Jane gave Rebecca a hug then together they sat and waited for Nancy and Stevie to come home.

175

They waited a long time until Jane became anxious. The snow was a few inches deep by now and the children should have been home earlier. 'Build up the fire, Beccy. I'm going to look for them.' First, Jane changed her clothes for something warm, and then stepped out into the cold.

She took the road to the village, peering into the dusk for the two children. The swirling snowflakes made it impossible to see far ahead. Soon she made out two dark shapes coming towards her.

'Where have you been all this time? You should have been home ages ago.'

Nancy was blowing on her frozen fingers. 'Suzy's Ma came for her and invited us to go to their house. It was light then. We had some cake and when we started for home it was snowing. Stevie was almost crying with the cold, weren't you, Stevie.'

The shivering boy murmured, 'My boots leak, Ma.'

'Come on, let's get you home as soon as we can.'

When they were all sitting around the fire, Nancy chatted about the party. Reaching into her pocket she brought out two little parcels. 'I brought yours for you, Beccy, and Stevie has his in his pocket.' The little parcels contained pieces of fudge and some lemon drops.

Jane asked if they were hungry but they all shook their heads. 'We had pie and some cake and cheese and bread.'

Jane had her eye on Stevie. He was lethargic and pale and had no interest in his parcel so she took him up to bed straight away, glad that the room at last was watertight even if not very warm.

The days passed and January rolled into February. Arthur turned out to be a man of habit and mostly turned up on Wednesday afternoon. He made suggestions as to what they might do together but Jane always declined, saying the children could not be left, especially Stevie who was not coping with the winter as well as she hoped. Arthur often brought some vegetables or a piece of meat but the better diet seemed to have little effect on the boy.

One day Arthur turned up with an oil lamp. 'How can you see in the evenings with only candles? Tell me when you need more oil.' That day they went for one of their walks. 'Are you mollycoddling that boy of yours, Jane? If he were mine he'd be in the fields with the men.'

'I reckon that would kill him, Arthur. He's not strong, but he'll pick up in the spring,' Jane said with some resentment. Arthur had always looked askance at her son, showing little sympathy with Stevie's frail form and lack of energy. Jethro was quite different and was always concerned for the boy, even though he rarely saw him. They walked in silence for a while then Arthur said, 'How about an answer, Jane? I am a patient man but time is getting on.'

'I'm sorry, but I have too many worries to consider the question. The price we get for the plait is so low and I'm told it is because the hat manufacturers are buying cheap imports. I am trying to think of some other way of earning.'

'You have only to marry me and all your worries would be over,' he declared. 'There would be no need for you to earn at all.' His louder voice told her of his frustration.

Jane's heart sank. She had been coping alone for so long that a life dependent on Arthur, or any man, held no attraction. She had to admit that at the present time she was dependent on his, and Jethro's, generosity, but she could not deny that it often rankled. However, to submit to another's authority was quite different from accepting gifts from friends.

'Arthur, I can see you are fed up with me and you know how much I value your friendship but I cannot contemplate marriage yet. Our present relationship is as much as I can manage at the moment. Don't you think it would be best for you to forget about me altogether and find yourself a more available woman?'

'There is no other for me. I am also a stubborn man and I shall not give up. I shall make you change your mind in time.' His firm expression told her no arguments were possible.

Jane battled with confused feelings. She did not welcome Arthur's attention yet dared not reject him out of hand. The more she knew of him the more sure she was that he would not react well to her true feelings. She knew she was exploiting him, and thought it wrong of her when she wanted to send him away forever. So far she was sure that Arthur had no inkling of her relationship with Jethro and the deceitful game disturbed her but what else could she do? They had been so careful, making sure that no sign of his visits was left behind for Arthur to find. However, with the lengthening of the days it was getting harder to be sure their secret was safe as he had to come so much later in the evening.

Not knowing what else to do, Jane had no option but to go on juggling the two relationships. How long could they go on? She thought she would just die if Jethro didn't come. Last time he had brought seeds for the garden. He sometimes brought a newspaper, the *Mercury*, and she began to learn what went on in the world beyond the village. Her interest lay mostly in the advertisements and sometimes there were stories that she read to the children. After, Stevie had to cut the paper into squares for the privy as soon as she had read it.

'There is going to be a census at the end of March,' Jethro told her. 'We all have to be counted.'

'Another one? I remember the last time. I was eighteen and had just married Dan.'

'Well, this time they want more information.'

'We won't have to go anywhere, will we, just like in the Bible?'

'No, a form to fill in, I think.'

'What about those in the Workhouse, and the homeless? They come to the door sometimes, thin and hollow-eyed, and in rags, looking for food or work. Mostly Irish, they tell me, fleeing from the famine there you told me about. I give them some bread if I can spare it, and direct them to the vagrants' place in the Hitchin Workhouse.'

'They won't get much there, for they have no legal right to be here. We badly need labour on the farm but the Irish are weak and half-starved and filthy. They are no good as workers. They have no knowledge of our farming methods for over there they grew only potatoes.'

'Yes, I read about it in the *Mercury*.' Jane said. 'It said they carry typhus and pass it on to our people.'

'All the good men who leave us are going to the towns to work in the factories where they can earn all year round. I would do the same, for I'm tired of work in the fields, but I can't leave my Da until things pick up. I'm hard put to think what I could do in Luton, or maybe Dunstable. Thomas might help, of course.'

'Dan used to say the same, yearning to better himself but with the children it was too late for him.'

'I want to go to the Great Exhibition but I bet Da won't let me go. Thinks it will put ideas in my head, I suppose.'

'What is this Exhibition?' she asked.

'It's in London, a big glass building.'

'Really, all made of glass?'

'Glass and iron. They've been building it for months. It's very big.'

'Why do you want to go?'

'I want to see what's there, Jane. It will have all the things that this country makes, for we are the best in the world at machinery, cotton, pottery, oh, every kind of industry. I want to see if there is anything there I can do. I'm sure to find something.'

'But what will your father say?'

'I don't care. I won't tell him.'

Jane was lost in thought for a long time. It was not too late for Jethro to look for advancement. If he did not go soon he would be stuck as Dan had been. He might not stay because of his father but because of her and in time, as he grew more discontented, he would regret it and perhaps blame her. 'You must stand up to your father. You have your own life to lead.'

'If I did leave here for good, would you come with me? We could have a better life together than this.'

'But the children, Jethro. It would be better if you go first and make your way. Then I would join you if a home and schools were possible. I would hate it if you went but if you must…'

'I cannot go without you, Jane, so I will stay. If I go I am afraid my Da will persuade you.'

'That will never happen, Jethro. I want only you.'

CHAPTER 16

The money Jane brought home from the plait market was less than before and the word around was that the situation would get worse. Jane racked her brain to think of some way to earn a little more. Already the family were relying on what Arthur and Jethro brought her, each of them unaware of the other's generosity, but it could not go on. At last she asked Rebecca to make some more of the pincushions she had made for her at Christmas.

'It was very pretty, Beccy, and I can still smell the lavender. We might sell them in the village and make a few shillings.'

'I'd like a change from plaiting, Ma, but we have no lavender until later on.'

'We can stuff them with something else. I have some bergamot, and some of the herbs I dried in the summer still smell strong. We could shred some of the wool left over from the hats I made for you as filling. What do you say?'

Rebecca said she would try one and was eager to start at once. She cut some heart shapes out of old material and spent the afternoon stitching them together. When stuffed with wool soaked in bergamot, the final result was deemed a success. The next pincushion had a fringe of ribbon lace and she had embroidered *Good Luck* on one side.

The question was how to sell these if they could make enough to make the effort worthwhile. 'Let us make a dozen and see if we can sell them in the village. You make the cover, Rebecca, and I'll stuff them and sew up the open edge. That way we should make them quicker.' Jane and Rebecca worked together and before long they had a variety of individually decorated and multi-coloured pincushions. Jane laid them out on a tray and on a fine afternoon they all walked to the village.

At first they planned to visit all the houses but then realised the haberdasher's shop might be interested in selling for them. It was a small shop run by Mrs Bunty

Brooks who was pleased to have this new line of merchandise and undertook to display and sell them for three pence each.

'I'm very grateful, Bunty.' After a moment she added, ' And to Rebecca for she has done most of the work.'

When they returned to the shop a week later, all the pincushions had gone. Jane collected two shillings and promised to supply the shop with more in a few days' time.

'Ma, I've had an idea,' Rebecca said as they walked home. 'Some people will use the cushions among their clothes for the nice smell. Other women want to strap the cushion to their wrist so they can use the pins easily as they sew. We could sew a ribbon on the back to tie round their wrist.'

Jane thought this an excellent idea but suggested a button and buttonhole for easier fixing. 'I don't know about you, Beccy but tying a ribbon to your wrist with one hand is so difficult.'

'They will take longer to make, Ma.'

187

'Then we shall ask for more money, say four or even five pence each.'

Sewing a buttonhole in a ribbon, even a wide one, proved difficult but soon they had two separate items for sale at two different prices. Jethro was much amused when he saw them and was impressed with their industry. Now Stevie had bits of cotton and cloth to sweep up and much less straw, though Nancy was still plaiting, for Jane was teaching her the finer plait for which she earned a little.

The cottage became a hive of industry but after they had sold their second lot, they found that the sales in the village fell away. 'You need a wider market,' Jethro told her. 'Why not bring some to Luton on Mondays? The haberdasher's shop there is bigger than Mrs Brooks'.'

Delighted with his suggestion, the next time she had a selection of pincushions prepared, Jane braved Mrs Turnbull's haberdashery shop in Luton and came back with a tentative promise of sales. She noted also the pretty materials, cottons and ribbons available there if she had the money to spend. 'She is going to sell them at five pence each,' Jane told Rebecca, who opened her eyes wide. 'Really, so much?'

'People have more money in Luton and we must not sell ourselves short, Beccy.'

After this, they applied themselves with renewed vigour to the task. New ideas surfaced all the time. New embroidered mottos, fancy stitching round the edges, and little rosettes made out of gathered ribbon all made the cushions attractive and each one different from the rest. Jane and Rebecca worked long hours, as long as they had plaited, but the work was creative and variable so they enjoyed it more. To start with they cut up any old clothes they had and then, when there was nothing left they could spare, Jane used some of their earnings and came home with a bundle of patchwork squares in many different patterns and colours, cut and prepared for any women skilled in the craft of patchwork quilting.

'She let me have it on tick,' she told her daughter. 'And I noticed she has many ribbons and ribbon lace too.'

The work of the household had to go on. Food had to be cooked and clothes had to be washed. The many scores of plait the three of them had done previously had dwindled to only what Nancy could do and she wanted to sew pincushions like her sister. 'I can do it, Ma, really I can.'

'We must keep up the plaiting, Nancy. It is too soon to rely only on something new. If they fail we will have no income at all. I'm going to plait as well, you know, when I can, so we will do it together.'

But Nancy was not happy and imposed a lengthy sulk on her mother and sister.

All around the area, families were working harder as the price of plait fell. Some were turning to bonnet sewing but most sank into a greater level of poverty and despair. Fewer children went to the plait school, for the older ones found work where they could: bird scaring, running errands, foraging, weeding, anything that would bring in a few pennies. Until harvest time, men's wages were stuck at about eight shillings a week and the price of food went up. Jane saw all this and felt glad to have developed this second string to her bow.

Time wore on, full of work and anxiety. As spring advanced, the weather warmed, and the seeds in the garden began to grow. Work on the farms picked up but there was no increase in the price of local plait. By May, all nature was lush, green and colourful, all wildlife busy with young, bees pollinating blossom, lambs in the fields, birds to and fro to their nests.

Jane was anxious, watching each month for confirmation that she was not pregnant. It was the time when she thought she was most likely to bring disaster on her lover and her own family. She and Jethro did their utmost to be safe, first with half a lemon, then with a netted sponge and careful washing. As she sewed the pincushions, counted them and calculated the gains, she thanked her lucky stars that so far all was well.

As the need to expand their market grew, they started a new product which also proved a success. Irritation with the number of flies which invaded their room made covers necessary for jugs and basins. She cut circles of cloth in several sizes, hemmed them with lace from which beads were strung to weight the cover over the rim of a vessel. They sold well and were quick to make.

By now there was a little more money to spend and some also to put in the tin on the shelf. Jethro was restless in his mind even while busy with farm work. Jane thought nostalgically of the nights when they would sit opposite each other by the glowing logs of the fire, a single candle on the shelf and their ankles entwined as they talked. By May they did not feel so enveloped in the safety of the dark, nor was there need of a fire except to boil water for tea.

As May advanced and a flush of green overtook the brown of ploughed soil, Jethro came, exhausted by a day of hedging or clearing ditches. 'I've made up my mind, Jane. I'm going to London.'

A stab of alarm went through her even though she had been half expecting that one day he would do something to vary the monotony of his farm work.

'I'm going to see the Great Exhibition. You won't see me for a few days.'

A few, how few? 'Has your Da agreed, then?'

'No, I shan't tell him. I shall just go when I've collected enough money together.'

She asked him when that was likely to be and he told her not for a month or so because it was too expensive to go so soon after the opening of the Crystal Palace. 'The entry price is lower now but I shall have the travelling to pay for and a place to stay for two days at least. I can't ask my father for extra money so I must save my wages.'

His eyes shone with excitement at the thought. 'People from all over the country will be going. I shall travel on the railway, Jane. Think of it.'

'But... but what do you hope to see, Jethro?'

'I want to see the big glass palace and perhaps the Queen but mostly all the things that this country makes – machinery, steam engines, cloth, pottery, oh everything. It is to show the world that our industry is the best. There will be something there that I can do and I am sure to find it there.' He paused, staring into the remains of the fire, his head full of anticipation.

Jane's alarm grew. She had encouraged him to stand up to his father but what if he found what he was looking for and never came back? She knew about city life, her father had told her. Rich people lived there, in their big houses and fine clothes. There was danger in the crowded streets where rich and poor mingled. There were horses, trams, coaches, carts and many opportunities for the capable and strong like him to succeed, but many dangers too. But he had to go and she would not try and stop him.

It was four weeks later that he told her it was all arranged. First he would go the Dunstable where his cousin Thomas would take him to the nearest station. From there he would travel in an open-topped railway carriage to London. He would find a lodging house near to the Hyde Park. He would see everything and in two days he would be home.

Arthur turned up at her door the day after Jethro had gone. He bustled into the cottage, his face a picture of frustration.

'What is it, Arthur? You look troubled,' she said, taking his cap and hanging it on the nail by the door.

'It's that son of mine. He's just taken off somewhere, left the milking, and the weeding in the root field, and the horses. I had to do everything, the blighter. He just upped and left me with all his work to cover.'

'Do you have no idea where he has gone?' Jane asked innocently.

'Left me a note. *Back soon*. I ask you. All I know is his Sunday clothes are gone. Some woman, I shouldn't wonder. He's been holding things mighty close to his chest lately so I thought something was up. If he's gone off to marry some strumpet, I'll kill him.'

'I expect he'll turn up in a day or two. Don't worry.'

But Arthur grumbled on and wouldn't let the matter drop.

CHAPTER 17

Four days later, in the late evening, Jane heard a gentle tap on her window and knew that Jethro was back. He clasped her to him as soon as she let him in and they kissed and hugged as if they had been separated for weeks. 'I've missed you so much,' she murmured. 'I was worried that London life and its ways had persuaded you to stay.'

'No, never, my dearest one. How could you think that of me? But it was an amazing time and I saw so much. The Palace is so big with so many pavilions I couldn't manage to see them all. There were things, amazing things, from all over the Empire. And there were thousands and thousands of people, rich and poor, all milling around, inspecting the displays. You'd have been amazed, Jane, at the size of the city, the noise, the bustle, the wide streets and big houses. It was a wonder.'

Jane watched the excitement light up his beautiful face and she thought: *I have lost him*. How could the small affairs of their tiny village, the backbreaking labour of the farm and she herself have any attraction for him now that he knew what was beyond? She pulled him to a chair and asked what else he had seen. The Queen, perhaps? There was a tremulous surge of feeling inside her, hard to identify, and she needed time. 'Tell me more,' she urged.

'I saw the Koh-i-Noor diamond, the biggest in the world and I used a new flush toilet for inside houses. You had to pay a penny and then pull down a handle to make everything flush away. I saw the biggest steam hammer in the world and machines for everything you could think of. Oh, and a great lump of gold weighing several pounds, tapestries from France and enormous urns from Russia.' He sat back, overcome with the overwhelming variety of all he had seen.

They were silent for a moment and Jane was afraid a distance had opened up between them. Did he feel it too? Was he now the same Jethro after all this strange experience, all this new knowledge of the world?

Jethro stirred, then added, 'I brought you and the girls something. They are on the step.' He got up, opened the door and picked up a package. 'I wanted you to have something beautiful.'

Holding her breath, Jane opened the parcel. Inside was a velvet shawl in a rich dark red, fringed with gold thread and embroidered with coloured birds and flowers. She held it out, feeling the luxurious softness of the material. 'Oh Jethro, it is so beautiful.'

'Not as beautiful as you. I had to bring something small to carry. There are two caps in there for the girls, one each. I hope they like them.'

Jane pulled out a white and a pink cap, made of fine muslin and silk that she knew the girls would love and finally a wooden soldier standing straight to attention for Stevie.

Jane laughed when she saw it. 'He's never seen a real soldier though I showed him a picture in the newspaper.

He'll be so excited. Thank you, Jethro, I hope these didn't cost you a lot of money.'

'Only the best for you, dearest,' and they kissed again.

As they lay together on the day bed a long time after, Jane asked the one overwhelming question. 'And did you see your future there, among all those displays?'

He rolled away from her and stared at the ceiling. 'I saw all these machines from all over the country and they were a mystery to me. I realised that all I know about is farming. I recognised things that we could make use of here, things to speed up the work, make everything more efficient and not so back-breaking.'

'What sort of things?'

'Well, we still sow by broadcasting the seed by hand. I saw a seed drill that can do that job much faster. We still use the scythe on the barley and it takes a team of men to cut a field. There was a reaping and threshing machine that can do the work of twelve men and so many other machines. Some were for muck spreading. Some of our stuff is just as it has been for generations.'

He paused. 'Of course they all cost money and Da hasn't got beyond the steam engine that comes at harvest time. I don't think he would know where to buy these even if he could afford them.'

'You could enlighten him.'

He chuckled. 'Oh yes, you can imagine how that would go. He thinks the old ways are best.' He turned to her again. 'But enough of all that, tell me how your work is doing.'

So Jane told him that sales were very slow but she was saving a little money. The pot covers were popular for the summer and they had started ladies' handkerchieves with embroidered flowers which Nancy had turned her hand to without a word to her mother.

He enquired about Stevie, and she told him the boy was useful in the house and went foraging for hedge fruits and herbs when the weather was fine. He was still very thin but cheerful and loved to clown to make them all laugh as they worked.

After Jethro had gone, Jane stroked the soft velvet of the shawl. Where would she ever be able to wear such a rich garment? It glowed in the lamplight and the birds and flowers sparkled but it was out of keeping with everything they possessed and would surely arouse talk if she were to venture out in it. It would not do to hide it away, however, so she hung it between two hooks on the wall opposite the window where it would glow in the sunlight and she knew it would raise her spirits even on the gloomiest days.

Arthur turned up a couple of afternoons later. 'My oh my, where did you buy that?' he said on entry and Jane kicked herself for not removing the shawl.

'Oh that?' she said, pretending surprise. 'It was a gift.'

'So who has enough money to give you a gift like that?'

Jane turned away and busied herself with the stitching. 'From a grateful customer. Someone I helped. They didn't want it.' She knew she was blushing so kept her face averted.

He walked up to the shawl and fingered a corner. 'Looks new to me. Never been worn, I'd say.'

'Really? I don't know about that.' Change the subject, she thought. 'Is Jethro back yet?'

'Aye, turned up yesterday. Been to Dunstable to visit his cousin, my brother's boy, it seems. Filled his head with a load of nonsense by all accounts. Why he couldn't say where he was off to beats me.'

'Not marrying a strumpet then.'

'No, thank the good lord for that.' He stood gazing at the shawl with a slight frown, then after a moment of musing, looked away. 'You ready for a walk, Jane?'

'Could the girls come too? It is such a lovely day.'

The frown deepened. 'That is not in our agreement. Let them go when we come back.'

Later that afternoon, Jane warned the children. 'I don't want anyone to know Jethro brought those gifts for us so keep that information to yourselves, right?'

'Why, Ma?' Stevie said.

'Because people might be jealous and want him to give them gifts too.'

'Do you mean Mr Ward as well?'

'Especially Mr Ward.' She noticed Rebecca kept her eyes lowered and her lips tight shut as if she fully understood the situation.

Jane later discovered that Arthur was not convinced by her 'gift from someone she helped'. Nor was he convinced by his son's claim to have visited his cousin. 'I could kick myself,' Jethro told her. 'I've put you in a difficult position. But I'm tired of the secrecy, the lies, and the creeping in late at night. Why does my loving you have to be such a hole-in-the-corner affair? I want the whole world to know.'

'Yet you also know that the day your father discovers the truth, the sky will fall in,' Jane said.

Jethro shook his head sadly. 'I know, I know. He'll kick me out, that's for sure.'

These words resounded often in Jane as she worked. She took down the shawl and hid it away but Arthur never commented on its absence. One day as Jane sat by the window, she paused in her sewing and gazed out. It was Wednesday and she was expecting Arthur to visit as usual. Usually she saw him come along the lane from the track to her door but as she looked she could see him standing in the lane. Jessie was talking to him and she wondered why he bothered to listen to the gossip she was inevitably telling him. He kept glancing towards the cottage as he listened and from his serious expression she thought he looked impatient to be away. Putting her work to one side she got up to await her visitor. She waited, standing by the door for several minutes but he never came. She glanced through the window to check but there was no sign of either Arthur or Jessie.

Jane's mind played around with possible reasons for Arthur's non-appearance. Jessie had reminded him of something and he'd hurried home? He had suddenly felt unwell? Jessie had complained and he'd gone with her to investigate some issue? But underneath all these thoughts was the awful suspicion that Jessie had been telling him of her neighbour's nightly visitor. Jessie might be a slattern but she wasn't stupid. She could keep watch after dark and draw her own conclusions about the identity of the mystery gardener and his lengthy times indoors afterwards.

Suddenly, Jane was impatient to tell Jethro what had happened and that it was likely that Arthur had suspicions even if he did not know for sure. He was likely to call later as darkness fell, and she fidgeted and tapped her foot until then. When the children had gone to bed, she paced the room, she stood, then sat, crossing and uncrossing her legs as the hours went by. When at last she admitted to herself that he was not coming, a new worry started. Had Arthur had words with Jethro, perhaps quarrelled with him? Had his father forbidden Jethro to come? If so, she couldn't see Jethro complying with that order at his mature age. Whatever had happened up at the farmhouse was a direct result of Jessie's interference. In some ways it was a relief, for now there need be no more secrecy, no more deceit, but she had to know.

Jane stayed up late, thinking that whatever had delayed Jethro would not stop him coming no matter how late it was. When she finally did retire, she lay awake into the early hours until she heard a knocking on her door. She was up in a flash and down the steps, feeling her way in bare feet. The moon was bright and a cold light lit up the downstairs room. Jethro stood at her door as she had guessed.

Urgently, he bent to whisper, 'I know it's late Jane but I had to come.'

He looked harassed and she could see at once that he was dressed for travel and her heart sank. She reached to pull him over the threshold.

'He knows all, Jane. Someone told him. I suspect your neighbour… and he's kicked me out – locked the doors against me.'

Wide-eyed, Jane put her hands over her mouth. The worst had happened 'Is he so very angry?' Because of the hour they were whispering to each other.

'Oh indeed, he is angry but mostly determined to be rid of me. I spoke up in my… well, our defence, but the blame is all mine and he won't have me around a day longer. I must go.'

'But where? Where will you go, my darling?' Jane was trembling with either the chill of the night or her shock.

'To Dunstable to see Thomas first, but I have to go now. I am to take nothing from the farm so I must walk.'

'Oh dearest, you could stay here till morning when transport is possible.'

'I dare not, Jane. If that neighbour was to find out, your reputation would suffer and I cannot allow that.' He was talking fast, walking up and down the room, his arms flying here and there in agitation.

Jane caught his arm and urged him to sit for a while. 'But Jethro, what will you do for money?'

He gave a false laugh. 'No problem there. He threw money at me and I almost didn't take it, I was so furious, but then I reconsidered.'

'Do you think that in a while maybe he will relent and have you back? How can he manage the farm without you?' She could not bear the thought that he would be gone for long.

'I'm not coming back, except for you. But will you wait for me, Jane, no matter how long it will be?'

Wringing her hands in anguish, what could she say but 'Always and forever, my darling. I shall be here no matter how long it takes.'

'Then that is all I care about. Now I must go, for the dawn is not many hours off.'

By the door they pressed close, their arms entwined, their kisses feverish in this last embrace. Then he broke away, driven by sorrow and desperation.

Jane stood in the open doorway in her nightgown, ghostly white and her heart aching as she watched him disappear into the shadows and away.

CHAPTER 18

By morning Jane was a wreck, having lain awake most of the night, her thoughts alternating between fear for Jethro and for herself. In her mind's eye she could see him striding alone through the deserted streets. All day, she was preoccupied, could not eat and was short with the children. Friday and Saturday were as bad. She would have liked to talk to Silvie but even she did not know how far the affair with Jethro had progressed and would have been shocked to hear it.

On Sunday afternoon, Jane hustled everyone up to Wards Wood. There were tense moments as they trooped past the farm but all was quiet. The children did what they usually did but Jane sat, gloomy and bereft. The children were quiet going down the path home, believing their mother's disappointment was because Jethro had not come.

Jane prepared to walk to Luton on Monday morning. She collected all the things she hoped to sell, supposing that her lift would not arrive. However, the cart stopped outside the cottage and for an instant her heart lifted. But it was Tom driving. 'Got to give you a lift to town,' he said as she came out.

'Jethro usually takes me. Why have you come?' she blurted out, eyeing the usual load of eggs and vegetables he was carrying.

'I dunno. I gotta do the market run and give you a lift. Those'r my instructions.'

Jane climbed aboard, determined to see if he had information about what went on at the farm. Tom sat with a blank face and she waited a moment as they moved off, considering whether he really had anything to say. Possibly he had no idea what went on behind the doors of the farmhouse? 'Thanks for picking me up,' she said. 'Didn't you see Jethro yesterday?'

'Not as I recall,' he answered, leaning forward to flick the reins.

She had always been on good terms with Tom. Normally he was a chatty fellow and she knew his wife, Dotty, although the family lived at the very far end of the village. The clop of the horse's hooves came loud as they passed down the road. She wondered if he had been told to tell her nothing. 'What about Arthur, isn't he concerned about where his son is?'

'Not as I noticed,' came another evasive reply.

She said, 'Is Arthur... well?'

'Oh, HE's all right.' Tom gave a short laugh. His tone was uplifted, implying that others weren't.

She rocked forward on the wooden seat and groaned. 'I fear that something terrible has happened to Jethro.'

Now Tom looked at her, concern on his face. 'Why should you think that?'

'Well, he's disappeared, hasn't he?' She wrung her hands and pretended to wipe a tear from her eyes. Perhaps a sign of her distress would persuade him.

After a thoughtful pause, he said, 'He's gone, Jane.'

'Gone? Gone where?'

'There was a spat at the farm on Wednesday night and his Da turned him out.'

'He turned him out of the house?' She blurted out the words to register her surprise.

Tom nodded. 'I didn't hear what it was about. I just heard the shoutin' and Jethro was gone in the morning.'

Jane looked at the passing trees, their branches reaching over the road. Her voice trembled as she asked, 'Has he gone for good, do you think?'

'No, idea. And I'm not supposed to be tellin' you this. Arthur's orders.'

'Thank you for telling me, Tom. I imagine Arthur must be very angry.'

He laughed. 'From what I heard, Jethro weren't too happy either, but he gave as good as he got.'

Jane sat transfixed. So, at last she had some idea of the row. They rode on in silence until they reached the outskirts of Luton.

'I'll drop you here, Jane, and pick you up from this spot,' Tom said, pulling the horse to a stop.

'Are you going to give me a lift every Monday?' Jane asked as she climbed down.

'Guess so. That's what the boss said,' and he flicked his whip lightly over the horse's back and they moved off.

PART TWO

CHAPTER 19

Weeks passed and Jane waited but didn't know what she was waiting for. She knew it was hopeless to expect her lover's tap on her window and there was no comfort now in her days. Despite the work and the children, she was suddenly lonely. An empty space had opened up in her world, all warmth, all happiness gone. She told herself stories: Dunstable wasn't far – he was waiting; he was working on a neighbouring farm and could return at any time. In her worst moments she pictured him walking the streets of some town, hungry and cold, not daring to return, but these were fantasies that depended on her fluctuating mood.

Sometimes she thought about Arthur, who did not come. She was glad he stayed away. Did he know what devastation he had caused her? He must know she was not thinking well of him and he did not care.

Determined to assert his rights like an old-time patriarch, he had cleared away a rival who just happened to be his son. She might claim he was jealous of the younger man but he would never admit it. Nor could she ever voice these thoughts, for as her income diminished, his support was more and more necessary.

As her earnings from the plait became less and less, it was almost pointless to go every week with Tom on Mondays. She went nevertheless, to take a few pincushions and pot covers to the haberdasher's. She stopped questioning him and only tried to keep up with the news from the farm. They were short of hands for the seasonal work. Ivor, Silvie's husband, could do less work because his back was in a bad way. The price of crops fell and the few boxes that came for them from the farm contained less when they depended on the gifts more.

After three weeks of Arthur's absence, Jane's anger had subsided into a weary depression. On the third Wednesday, he knocked on her door. She opened it wide then turned away, leaving him to come in if he wished.

'Good day, Jane, I hope you are well. I've been tied up at the farm lately but I hope Tom has been doing what I asked to help you with the travelling.'

These were pleasantries she had no time for. She wanted him to know how she felt about what he had done. 'I would prefer Jethro.' She spoke boldly, glancing swiftly at him then picking up her plaiting.

'Ah yes, well he's taken off. I thought he would at some point. All these young bloods do, you know. I did my best to keep him working for me but they all want to see the wider world, make their fortune.'

She paused to look at him. 'Are you telling me you had no hand in his going?'

Arthur studied her as he thought. 'Well, we did have a few words about one thing or another, I'll not deny. But he's not been content on the farm for some time. Reckoned he was too good for it. Always had these dreams about bettering himself, so I told him to go. I didn't want no discontent among the men so he weren't no use to me. If he thinks he can do something better, then he should go and do it, say I.' He paused, looking around him, talking quickly as if there had been no dispute.

'So that was the only reason you made him go?' Jane turned a mock innocent face to him. She might as well let him know she knew the truth.

He frowned and snapped back at her. 'If I did it was his cocksure belief in himself that forced matters. Too damn clever to follow the advice of his elders and betters. Tellin' me I was not doin' things right. Me with years of experience gotta give way to all these modern notions. If he thinks he knows better, let him take his ideas somewhere else.'

'Do you know where he's gone?'

'I don't, and nor do I care.' His frown cleared. 'Now Jane, I can see things are not good for you. What can I do to help?'

'You can tell that bastard, Silas Roberts to stay away from my door,' she burst out. 'He turns up from time to time, threatening me, moaning and groaning because I won't give him my plait. He's a pest and my girls are afraid of him.'

217

Silas had been on her doorstep that morning, not threatening this time but pleading, cajoling, making elaborate promises. He had wailed his unhappiness at her rejection, his loneliness and his ill luck because she was not by his side. Jane hadn't the energy to be rude to him. She shut the door on him, hearing from the path as he stepped back, 'You's my girl, you know that. You's my girl and you allus will be,'

Arthur said, 'I'll do what I can, Jane. Now, how about we take a walk like before?'

'Sorry Arthur, but if I don't finish these scores I'll have too little to sell on Monday.' And she showed him to the door.

Lifeless and bored, Jane went through her days, sewing and plaiting, cleaning, cooking, like an automaton. At night her body ached for Jethro and she wept silently for him until over time she felt she was weeping for someone as insubstantial as a dream.

When Arthur called again he was cheerful and talked only of the farm and how the year's wheat and barley would be. Jane listened to the talk until she could wait no longer and she broke in. 'Have you heard from Jethro? Do you know where he is?'

Arthur stopped and looked sourly at her. 'I told you I don't know where he has gone. Become a beggar, I reckon, since he enjoys living so dangerously. But as I was saying, I would like it if you came to the farm on Sunday. Bring the children. We shall have a tea and you will see how I live now.'

What did Arthur mean by that? Was his life so much better or worse than before? Did Jethro's absence make a difference that he wanted her to know of?

He could see the reluctance in her face. 'Come, come, it will be a treat for the children. I guess they never go anywhere but Ward's Wood and there's nothing there, is there?'

The barb stung. If he was going to taunt her, she would not bear it, and so she turned away.

He turned to the children sitting around the table. 'You all would like to have a tea at the farm, wouldn't you?'

Shyly, three heads nodded, so the die was cast. They would go to the farm on Sunday.

The family had all viewed the farm from outside the gate, the farmhouse on the other side of the yard and the run- down outbuildings grouped around. Behind the house rose the huge barn with other buildings, and beyond that were fields of wheat fields and barley, fields of root crops and grazing meadows for the cows and horses.

Arthur was waiting by the gate, neatly dressed and smiling. He welcomed them in.

Jane wasn't so very interested in the barns and sheds, the machinery, tools and implements Arthur seemed determined to show them, but she did notice how clean and tidy everything was. The milking parlour had been hosed down, the cow byre was empty of cows, the granary also empty and waiting the current year's harvest. There were great cart horses in the stables resting for the day with fresh hay and water. It appeared that every effort had been made to impress the visitors with the neatness and efficiency of the place.

The dairy was of some interest to Jane. There was a large butter churn, the handle turned by a girl of about Rebecca's age. There were milk churns and cream jugs around the room and butter moulds on the shelves. And she showed some interest in the cider press, never having been close to one before. 'Too early yet for apples,' Arthur said, waving his hands over a huge trough. 'I'll bring you some cider when we get going here.'

But it was when they finally went into the farmhouse that Jane's eyes went everywhere. The bread oven by the stove and a hotplate over the fire made her envious, as did the dresser with a few blue and white dishes and plates, the copper pans hanging on hooks and the logs stacked in a recess. These things were familiar from her girlhood at home with her parents. There were geraniums on the window sill and beyond she could see hay ricks, some still whole, others waiting the new hay of the year.

The big table had been laid with a feast – there was no other word to describe what they saw. There were game pies, pickled eggs, a ham bone and a baker's cake beside a bowl of fruit. The children were pop-eyed at the variety of good things to eat. Invited to sit, they set to with a will with sugared lemon juice to drink. Jane ate well too and joined Arthur in a glass of beer. He had become a different man, joking and joshing with the girls.

After they had eaten, Arthur suggested they look over the rest of the house. First they viewed the laundry and other downstairs rooms, then all trooped up the stairs. Arthur opened one door. 'Come in here, you little ones. Come and see.'

It was a child's bedroom with a litter of toys on the floor. 'See what you can find in here.' Curious, the three advanced into the room. Stevie immediately dropped to his knees before ranks of wooden soldiers in red-painted uniforms. The girls wandered in, searching for girls' toys but found instead jigsaws and stuffed animals and skittles.

'They'll be busy in there for a while,' Arthur said, closing the door on them.

'Where did all those toys come from?' Jane asked, a germ of suspicion in her mind.

'Been in the attic for many a year,' he replied smartly and moved on to another bedroom, larger than the rest.

Jane nodded. He must have brought them all down to entertain the children which was a kind thought but then the extravagance of the meal, and the unusual cleanliness and tidiness of the farm made her begin to think otherwise. It was all a plan to bewitch her with his wealth. She knew that most of the time the farmyard and the milking parlour were inches deep in cow muck. Who had cooked all the food? It was surely not everyday fare. Remembering the clean floor of the kitchen, she pictured it as it must be daily, trampled all over with the muddy boots of farm labourers in for their breakfast or queuing up to collect their wages on a Friday.

In this larger bedroom she saw a four-poster bed covered with a patchwork quilt and lace trimmed pillows.

'Is this your bedroom?' she asked, wondering about the propriety of this invitation.

'Eh, no. This is where my dear wife and I slept together. Since she died, I sleep in another room and a smaller bed.'

Jane turned to leave, feeling that she was encroaching on an intimate part of his life that had nothing to do with her.

Standing outside the closed door he said, 'You know, Jane, this could all be yours. You have only to say the word. You and I are going to end up lonely old folks when we could be together.'

She looked down at the floor, noticing a crust of dust along the edge of the wall. This was not the reality of life on a farm. It would be herself turning the handle of that butter churn. She would be scrubbing the mud from the floors and cooking food for more than the family. She would be out in the fields with the men when it was all hands out before the weather broke. And then there was that four-poster bed and all that entailed, all in a house brimful with reminders of Jethro.

Jane took a breath to steel herself, and half turned away. 'Arthur, I am grateful that you should offer me all this but I cannot accept. I have other plans and I have the children to think of.'

'What plans? Were you thinking that my son will return? Think again, Jane, he is gone for good. He has other opportunities, that's if he is not already married and settled somewhere in foreign parts. Why do you waste time thinking of him when your chances are here now for the taking?'

'I know you think me contrary, but I can't help it.' In an agony of regret she shook her head.

'As for the children, I shall send them to proper schools. Their future will be better than any you can give them. And that boy of yours will grow hardy, I shall see to it.'

'You are very kind and I am an ungrateful woman, I know that, but no, Arthur. I can't accept.'

His face reddened at her words and she could see a clenched fist by his side. 'So you are going to keep me dangling like the last time. Think of it, woman, your

225

own kitchen, your own dairy and laundry, education for your children and fine clothes for yourself. How can you refuse me when no other woman in her right mind would?'

Jane clenched her hands together in real anguish. 'I know, I know, I am beyond understanding, but please don't make me feel worse than I do myself. I must go, we must go, for I have to think about this.' Turning, she opened the door and called to the children. 'Come, Rebecca, Nancy, Stevie, you must thank Mr Ward for his great kindness to us.'

Reluctantly, the children left the toys and stood in a row before Arthur. 'Thank you, Mr Ward for a lovely tea,' they chorused. The girls bobbed a curtsey and Stevie put his hands behind his back.

Arthur just stared at them, the smiles all gone. He turned and led them down the stairs to the kitchen. The clutter of the meal was still on the table, and taking up what was left of the game pie, he thrust it at Jane. 'Take the pie and the fruit,' he said brusquely. It would be rude to refuse so Jane took it and the girls carried the fruit.

Then they all trooped outside, through the yard and home.

CHAPTER 20

As they walked to the cottage, Jane asked herself if she was being wise. Was Arthur right and Jethro would never come back? Despite his assurances, there had been no word from him, nothing to sustain her through the long lonely days only made slightly better by the modest sales of their sewing efforts. But for how long could she rely on the children's help? Without their enthusiasm and preparedness to work all hours, she could not make enough to keep them all. Without Arthur's help they would fall into deeper poverty and without any man's protection, she would be prey to the likes of Roberts.

Could she live without love? There were some who laughed at the many romantic novels she had heard about. 'Unreal' was the most common comment. But to Jane, love was not unreal, it was the force that coloured a grey life, that made a heart sing and brought joy to bleak days.

'Can we have some more pie, Ma?' Stevie asked as they went inside their cottage.

'Dear me, no. You must still be full to the brim. Tomorrow perhaps, for breakfast. Now, Rebecca, light the lamp and I'll read you all a story before you go to bed.'

The weeks passed and still there was no word from Jethro. The vegetables in the garden grew large, which was just as well because there were no more gifts from Arthur Ward. He came, but he was not so cheerful and came empty handed, so Jane reckoned his visits were merely to check that she was as determined as before. Since the farm wasn't doing so well, Tom's lifts became more erratic until Jane couldn't rely on him any more. She supposed he was needed to do the work Jethro might have done. It left her with deciding whether to renew her deal with Roberts or walk to the market. She sold a few pincushions, handkerchieves and jug covers in the village but not enough to swell the few coins in her tin on the shelf. The girls managed to thrive on potatoes and veg from the garden but Stevie worried her. He was content and always helpful but was pale and tired easily.

The cycle of the seasons proceeded in their usual fashion. Life in the village went on, with another harvest, another thanksgiving, birthdays and Christmas. The waiting and hoping exhausted Jane. Her alternating periods of joy followed by depression affected the household, making the children too sombre, too quiet, and she could not bear it. She told herself that she was not a silly romantic girl any more. The business of making a living must continue although she felt a hardness creeping into her soul as a result of the continual struggle. On his infrequent visits, she was short with Arthur and rude with Roberts who would not stay away.

Eventually, not knowing when Tom would call for her, Jane went to call on Silvie and begged a favour.

'You don't have trouble with Roberts, do you, not with your Ivor often at home and your aunt living with you?'

Silvie shook her head. 'He knows better than to try it on with me. My aunt sits in that chair,' and she pointed to the elderly woman plaiting contentedly opposite the open door. 'And he would get short shrift from Ivor if he heard one whisper of his cheek. We all know what he's like.'

'If I brought my scores to you, could you pass them off as your own and give the money to me after? If I don't have that walk on a Monday I can do so much more.'

'I reckon Silas will wonder how we've managed to do so much more but I can tell him something. It's a good idea. Are you going to tell Tom not to come?'

'No, he'll be useful on the few occasions when I see him, when I've got things to take to Bunty to sell for me. And I have to go to pick up the money if she has managed any sales. I wish it were more often.'

Silvie nodded her understanding. 'I'll be happy to do that for you, Jane. Will you bring what you've got on Sunday afternoon after church? I'll enjoy watching Silas's face when he comes.'

The plan proved a good one for Jane. She would send the children to the stream by themselves. A pleasant visit to Silvie was preferable to an awkward meeting with Arthur as they passed the farm gate.

Stevie often took off by himself to forage for hedge food. He would come home with blackberries, crab apples, wild garlic, even nettles, and later as autumn advanced, picked mushrooms, and elderberries. All the youngsters in the village did the same, augmenting what could be grown in their gardens.

In early November he extended his range and went along the main road towards Luton. He came back later than usual with a tale of having met a family camping out under a hedgerow. 'They had made a little fire, Ma, and were cooking some gruel but they were very thin and raggedy. There was a Da and a Ma and a boy. I talked to him. He said they were Irish, come down from Leeds. He said his daddy was looking for work in the town and I told him it was Luton. He was even thinner than me.'

'Heavens, Stevie, you didn't stay too long with them, I hope. I warned you to stay clear, didn't I?'

'Yes, but the boy called to me and I was sorry for him, Ma. They were so tired and poor so I just talked with them for a bit and then I came home 'cos I was cold.'

It was not unusual to meet vagrants on the road to Luton with nowhere to go, but they seldom ventured as far as the village. They would be given some help in Luton but were moved quickly on from the village. Jane was sorry for them, destined to wander the roads, surviving how they could, a blight on the countryside but she was glad her cottage was outside the village proper and a good way off the main road, for the risk of infection was well known.

A few days later Stevie complained of a headache. He felt hot to the touch and the next day was sick after his breakfast of bread and lard. Jane had seen this before so she thought nothing of it, but a couple of days after, he had pains and was so clearly not well that she began to worry. She put him to bed in the daybed so that she could watch over him. She stoked up the fire to keep the room warm as he complained he was cold, although to her he felt feverish. She told the girls to keep their distance just in case he was infectious. Then the days of diarrhoea started, and the vomiting. When he threw off his blankets, she saw then the dark rash on his chest and her anxiety gave way to horror. She knew then what she was seeing: the Irish Fever. Hers was not the only child suffering for she had heard of others. When she thought of the likely outcome, her blood ran cold.

From that moment, all else was driven from her mind. She sat beside the bed, whispering, 'Stevie, sweetheart, be brave my darling boy. I'm here. I shan't go.' She stroked his hair away from the beads of sweat on his brow. 'Give me your hand. Hold on to me. Are you too hot?' She was racked with the pain of watching him struggle to breathe, her own sweet boy, his father's pride. She was glad that Dan was not here to see him grow weaker day by day, his skin almost transparent and his lips dry and cracked. Knowing they were all at risk, she kept the girls well away, but prayed that she herself was resistant. She begged bones from the butcher to make bone broth, and spoon by spoon, fed it through Stevie's parched lips. She applied cold compresses to drive down the fever, pressed water to his mouth but nothing made him feel any better.

She sat hunched in the chair hardly moving from the bedside, refusing food, growing more hollow-eyed from lack of sleep. Neither day or night made any difference to her. Rebecca was left to prepare scant meals and comfort a tearful Nancy. Jane sent Rebecca to Silvie with the news and the lengths of plait they had managed to complete.

Some people, the hale and hearty young and adults, survived the typhus but she knew it would be touch and go for Stevie, whose resistance was minimal. He had always been vulnerable although the better diet of earlier months had slowly improved him. Lately, as their income fell, they had all often been hungry. Jane herself had often given up her own food so that Stevie might have enough. Had he not caught the infection he might have made it like his sisters, but now Jane could see it was not to be.

In her darkest hours, Jane imagined she was dying too and felt an ill-defined anger at God or Fate and fury at her own helplessness. She reproached herself for all her recent absorption in her own happiness and believed what was happening to Stevie was retribution for her selfishness. There rose in her a fierce determination to protect her girls, her Rebecca, solemn and accommodating, and Nancy, bewildered at her brother's inability to mend.

The word spread around the village and the neighbours brought firewood and food. They were fulsome in their advice: cider vinegar, garlic, cloves, and in desperation Jane tried them all but to no avail. The word finally reached Arthur Ward. He came, carrying two pints of milk. Jane, haggard, uncombed and unwashed, nodded her thanks but could hardly force a word through her lips. Nor could Arthur say much as he was undermined by sickness of any kind and stood helpless and silent before the suffering boy.

Jane raged inside at the sight of him. What good was his wealth now? With all his confidence, what could he offer her now that could bring one jot of comfort? She was ready to turn on him should he make one comment about Stevie's former fragility or his own expectation of the child's poor resistance, but he said nothing. He just turned to go, nodding to the girls as he went.

Day by day, Stevie faded until he lay unmoving and silent. Jane lay a hand on his chest but could feel no movement and after a while she knew he was gone. For long moments she covered her face with both hands, leaning forward, wanting to rest her head on the thin body but stopping in time. Then she stood and looked down at him, a sob escaping into the silence. Both girls stood together on the far side of the room, afraid in the face of this moment, not knowing what they should do or say.

Soon Jane turned to them, her face taut with the effort of control. 'Girls, I must go and fetch Silvie and the vicar. Sit quietly till I come back.' And she went out into the drear November day.

CHAPTER 21

Stevie lay in his coffin for days before the vicar could bury him. Rebecca and Nancy put flowers all around him and fresh ones on the day when he was carried to St Peter's small churchyard. Later, Jane could hardly remember much of what followed for she moved in a mindless daze. It was a confused time but some things she would never forget: the small coffin with the still figure in the white grave clothes given by the vicar, their room made dark by the covered window and the laurel wreath on the door warning all comers of a death in the house. She remembered the small cluster of mourners at the graveside, the vicar urging her to pray when she could not. And the undercurrent of grief which dogged Jane's every waking moment for many weeks after.

Other people lost children, of course they did, for it was common not only in the village for babies and the very young to die. Some even thought it 'churchyard luck' to lose a child and have one less mouth to feed.

Some babies were not named in their first year, so unsure was an infant's survival. But this was Jane's own grown child. This was her loss and her family's alone, shattering their former happy days. They could not afford the kind of memento that the better off people arranged but Jane cut off a lock of Stevie's hair to keep. One day she would buy a locket for it. At least Stevie did not have the shame of a pauper's burial and she silently promised him a headstone one day to mark the spot they planned to visit often.

The bleak winter weather mirrored Jane's mood. Though their small reserves of money allowed them to keep some of the mourning customs, it seemed as if the world around them was as depressed as they were. The summer and the year's harvest had been fair but by winter, wages had fallen low and if it rained, the menfolk were not paid at all. Even the women had worked for a time in the fields, lifting, topping and tailing turnips but they took home only half what a man would earn.

When Jane felt especially low she walked to the graveyard and stood by the little hump of soil enclosing her Stevie, not far from Dan's grave. Over the past year she had gone to talk to Dan less often but now she went to talk to Stevie. She would talk to him in her head. She had memories of him laughing at the table, sitting up grinning in the big bed, struggling to light a fire, but these glimpses were fading. The few dead flowers around him were now crisp and brown, blowing away in fragments into the wind. It was as if he were flying away from her, the memories disintegrating into slivers, leaving her with only one comforting thought, that now her boy was with his father. Sometimes she wondered how she could carry on when the loss of him crippled her, allowing her to go through the motions of a life pretending she was whole when she was not. It was only when she thought of her girls, firm, strong and vigorous, that her mood was restored to something resembling cheerfulness. They needed her to help them with their own loss and she would not fail them.

It was about that time that the girls started stitching handkerchieves with a black border but the returns were meagre. A joyless Christmas came and went and 1854 promised little good for anyone. By reports, even Silas Roberts was gloomy as families left the village to make better lives elsewhere. Times were hard for him too, for the hat manufacturers to whom he sold plait were now wanting imported finer and cheaper plait.

'Watcheroo, Jane, you still got your fiddle face on? You's strugglin' like us all, I sees.'

'That's enough of your blather, Mr Roberts.'

'Now why is you callin' me Mr Roberts, since we been so matey in the past? I know you's given up the plaitin' but I like to pass the time of day with my best girl.'

Jane folded her arms and leant against the door jamb. 'Go away.'

'Hang on there, I got an idea to put to you. You knows how far I travels to get my plait, and much good it's doin' me, I can tell you. Well, I hears how you is makin' sewn things for the shops. What say I take your goods along with me and sell 'em for you in the places where you never go? You never gets to Toddington, do you? Nor Tring or Hemel, nor the villages in between.'

'That's true.'

'Whaddya think, eh? I sells your stuff and bring you the money.'

Jane burst out laughing. 'You think I would trust you with anything of mine? You must be mad to think of it.'

'But I gotta branch out, Jane,' he said wrinkling his brow. 'There's not so much in the plait for me these days. I gotta grow my business somehow.'

Jane studied him. He looked genuinely concerned. It was a good idea if only suggested by someone she might trust. But not him, never him. He would sell her goods and pocket the money. She would never know what price he asked nor if he gave her all he got. 'Sorry Silas, nothing doing. Go away.' And she closed the door on him.

There was still no word from Jethro and only infrequent visits from Arthur. Jane had encouraged the girls to go to Sunday school and over time they began to enjoy their lessons there. After church, as the girls made their way home, she visited Stevie's grave, still swamped by the sadness that overcame her at these times but she would not forget him.

Often in her leisure hours, Jane thought about the halcyon days and nights they had all enjoyed together. Jethro had been with her but after an absence of a year she began to fear that she would never see him again. Every time she met Arthur she made a point of mentioning Jethro because she could not believe a father would not know or care where his son was or what he was doing. On the day when he gave her a lift in his gig to Luton, his irritation with her repeated queries welled up.

'Why do you keep going on about him?' he fumed. 'I don't know where the boy has gone. Nor do I want him back. He can go to the dogs for all I care, which is exactly what has happened I've no doubt. He's no skills but the fantasies in his head, precious little education and no money so if he's not lying drunk in some ditch, he's picking turnips for some other farmer somewhere.'

Jane buttoned her lip. Remembering the quickness and ambition of Jethro, the picture Arthur painted was unlikely to be true. But if Arthur knew anything of Jethro's whereabouts, he was not going to tell her.

They travelled on for a distance and then Arthur said, 'You know it looks like war, don't you?'

'What war?'

'There's trouble brewing in Russia, a place called Crimea. Papers are full of the Czar waving his sword over Turkey. We can't let him get away with it. We have to look after our trading routes.'

Jane had only the faintest idea where Crimea was, or even Russia except that it was a long way over the sea. 'I can't imagine it will make any difference to us, will it?'

'All our young men will go and fight. It's hard enough getting enough hands to work in the fields at the best of times. I've got two drunken clods sowing right now.'

'Would Jethro go and fight?'

'For crying out loud, shut the fuck up about Jethro!' he shouted.

Deep in thought, Jane wrapped her shawl tightly about her. If life was going badly for Jethro, a spell of soldiering might be an attractive prospect. It would be a chance to see something of the world. And if he survived the fighting, he would come back… if he survived… The thought brought a stab of anxiety. He might be wounded and if he couldn't work, he might end up a wandering vagrant, in poor health, begging like so many in the countryside these days. He would come back to her but he might only be a shell of a man then, if he came back at all.

They reached the outskirts of Luton and Arthur asked where she wanted to go.

'I want to visit Mary Turnbull. I have some materials to buy.'

'I'm meeting a fellow in the Lilley Arms. I'll drop you off there.'

It happened that as Jane alighted from the gig, Silas Roberts emerged from the door of the tavern. It was mid-afternoon and his face was ruddier than usual. He stood, his feet wide, and watched the gig move off, then stumbled across the road and grabbed her roughly by the arm.

'What's this? Who's that fellow you spendin' time with, drivin' around the town? I don't expect to see my girl hobnobbing with other fellas.' His speech was slurred and spit flew in every direction.

Jane shook her arm free. 'What's it to you, Silas Roberts, who I go with? It's none of your business.'

'Yus it is. No rich bod is takin' my place. We is partners, you and me.'

'Stop shouting, people are looking at you.'

'What do I care 'oo's lookin'. I won't 'ave it, do you 'ear? Oo is he?'

'He's a neighbour and a friend of mine.'

'A friend, eh. What sort of a friend?'

Jane's frustration at his presumption burst out of her. 'A good friend, a close friend, if you must know. Now leave me alone and let me get on with my shopping.' She knew he was staring after her as she marched away. His interference was not to be borne when she had so much else to worry about.

Mary Turnbull's shop looked depressingly short of useful stock when Jane entered and Mary was not as welcoming as in the past. 'Sorry Jane, but times are hard. No one has any money. I'll take some of your stuff but I can't promise much in the way of sales.'

'Well, I've brought some anyway. They will help fill your empty shelves.' Jane passed the box to Mary who said, 'I heard about your boy. So sorry, Jane. One less mouth to feed in this difficult time, I suppose.'

'I never thought of it like that,' Jane said, her voice bleak.

'No, of course not. But it's getting awful bad in this village. Move or starve seems to be what people are doing. I hear of empty cottages every day. And that Mrs

247

James, you know, the plait mistress, only has twelve kids to teach. You still plaiting? It's a dying art, Jane. No money in it now.'

'I know. I was hoping another string to my bow would make a difference. I know you've done your best for me but a few shillings now and again will not feed us.'

'What will you do?'

Jane shrugged her shoulders. 'What can I do?'

'I'm thinking of moving to Hitchin.'

Despairing, Jane looked around the almost empty shop. If Mary closed it, that would be the end of their sewing dream for she could not travel to Hitchin despite the possibility of a bigger market there. Nor was moving an option. What would Jethro do if he came back for her and found her gone? She had to stay and wait as she had said she would.

Two days later Roberts was again at her door. 'Tell me who this friend is so I can knock 'is block off.'

Jane groaned. When was she going to be free of this imbecile? 'Who my friends are is no concern of yours and you can forget all this partners nonsense. We are not partners and never have been. How many times do I have to tell you? I'm friends with whoever I like and I don't like you. I don't know what you are expecting but you are wasting your time.'

'As long as you's not thinkin' of marryin' this good friend of yorn.'

'I'll marry whoever I like and whenever I feel like it. And the quicker I do, maybe you will get the message and leave me alone!' She was shouting at him at the top of her voice, not caring who heard, but her words had a violent effect on him.

He called her a mad ungrateful bitch. He stamped and yelled and thumped his fist on her door jamb. He called her all the offensive names he could think of then abruptly adopted a wheedling tone, attempting to persuade her by bland words. It had no effect on Jane for her patience was at an end and she wished to be as cruel as necessary to have done with him.

As response, he said almost sorrowfully, 'You ain't marryin' anyone, Jane. You gave me the slip last time and it won't happen again. If I hears one hint of that happenin' I'll be round here with my shotgun, you understand?' For those last words, his voice took on a low menacing tone.

'It's no good you threatening me, you stupid old man. You had better watch out yourself. I've got people who would sort you out and make you sorry you ever came to my door. Now, off with you and don't come back!'

He growled and with much shaking of fists, spitting and glowering looks, he gave up. 'You'll be sorry, you see if you ain't. I know who put you up to this.'

When he had finally gone, Rebecca remarked how she had never seen Jane so cross. 'Do you really think he would bring a gun, Ma?'

Jane found herself stamping around the cottage in her anger. 'No, he's all talk. I'm not afraid of him. I hope I've finally got the message over to the great lump.'

Nancy looked up from her work and giggled. 'You was awful savage, Ma. I never heard you shout like that before.'

'I hope it did some good and we've seen the last of him. That's all I want,' Jane said, snatching up the garter she had been stitching. However, it was becoming clear that their situation was worsening by the day. There was no obvious outlet for their work and all the goodwill Jane had collected was being lost.

She sagged into a chair, suddenly tired, tired of being poor and the struggle and the worry about the future. It looked as if soon they would be even poorer than they had been before. It was hard to still the turmoil in her mind.

'Shall you both come with me to the village for a walk? I need to calm my nerves. We'll go to the churchyard and see Stevie.'

'But Ma, we went yesterday.'

'Yes, I know, dear, but I need to talk to him.'

CHAPTER 22

Arthur's next visit was unexpected and he appeared troubled. He slipped hastily through her door and then went to the window to peer up the lane. Jane put the kettle on the fire for tea, watching him fidget when he sat at her table. 'Where are the girls?' he asked.

'They are out back, staking the beans and weeding carrots. Why, what's the matter, Arthur?'

'Oh nothing, only I was approached in the town yesterday by a rough fellow I thought I recognised. He warned me he was on to me and I'd better watch out. I tried to delay him for an explanation but he got lost in the crowds.'

'Was that all?'

'At the time, yes, but I have seen him skulking in the village here and just now I swear I saw him at the door of that Jessie woman's cottage.'

'What did he look like?'

'Hefty, big-bellied, wearing a black bowler. '

'I know who he is. He's the local plait dealer, name of Roberts. I mentioned him to you before, remember? He's not usually around on a Wednesday though.'

'So what does he have to do with me?'

'Nothing, I imagine. Forget him, he's nobody.'

Arthur grunted and they began to talk of other things. After a brief pause he said, 'When are you going to marry me, Jane?'

Jane laughed briefly but she could see he was serious so she folded her arms on the table and looked soberly at him.

'I'm not ready for marriage, Arthur. I keep telling you.'

'So what are you waiting for? If you're hoping that son of mine will come back, then give up the idea. He's on his way to Russia to fight for England.'

Jane gasped and raised her head. 'Do you know that for certain?'

'That's what I hear.' He nodded and turned away.

Immediately, she was alert and cried, 'What do you hear? Who told you this?' Could she believe him or was it his way of stopping her bothersome questions?

'Oh, for God's sake, Jane, why can't you get on with your own life? You are getting older by the year. How long are you going to choose to live like this?' He swept his arm around the room.

Jane put her head in her hands. 'I'm sorry, you must think me a hopeless case.'

He reached out and took her hand, the first affectionate gesture she had ever seen him attempt.

'Look, Jane, you are the woman I want in my house. My choice out of them all. I'm willing to share all I have to make you content. Maybe I'm not your perfect choice but we must all compromise in life.'

Sadly and without a thought, the words burst from her. 'I was deeply in love with Jethro.'

He stared at her for a moment, then said, 'Was it because he was young? You know I can do nothing about that.'

Her voice wavered as she fought to hold back the tears. 'It was everything about him. It just happened and you sent him away.'

He was brisk in his reply. 'He didn't deserve to have you.'

'Surely only I can decide that.'

'What? Blinded by romantic ideas about love, were you in any fit state to decide what is best for you?'

Dumbly, Jane nodded.

Arthur stood up. 'Then I see I must rethink my plans. I won't wait forever for good sense to be restored to you. You cannot expect it, Jane, so take note of that.' He picked up his mug and drained the last of the tea, then grabbed his cap and left Jane to consider his words.

When the girls came in from the garden, Jane asked them if they had seen Mr Roberts at Jessie's cottage.

'Yes, we saw him. We saw her talking to him and then she let him inside,' Rebecca replied.

'How long did he stay?' But neither of the girls had seen him come out and go. Jane had the idea that she might catch him and warn him to stop stalking Arthur. She went out and wandered down their garden path and looked over at Jessie's cottage. Everything was quiet and there was no indication of whether Silas was in there or not. She bent low to deadhead some of the marigolds in the border and when she straightened up she saw Jessie's door open and Silas emerged, adjusting his clothing, his hat rakishly on the side of his head. She knew at once how long he had been closeted with Jessie and what he had been up to. She turned quickly to return indoors but he had seen her and yelled across, 'Jane Chapman, as I live and breathe.'

Jane stopped and turned, waiting as he approached, a smug, self-satisfied grin on his face. 'You's lookin' very fresh this afternoon.'

She almost commented on how exhausted he looked after his strenuous hour with Jessie but thought better of it. 'I want to know why you are harassing my friend.'

'Your farmer friend? I know who he is now. Mister Ward, ain't he. I told 'im to leave you alone. I told 'im you and me didn't need no rich bloke muscling in on our connection. I told 'im I had my eye on 'im and he'd better watch his step. Lives around 'ere, don't he?'

'Yes, he does, but you have no business threatening him. Why don't you mind your own business?'

'Because you and me, Jane...'

'There is no *you and me*. Just keep out of my affairs.'

'Aha, so it is an affair.' His face clouded over, the cheery smugness suddenly gone.

'Oh go away, Silas.' Jane hurried indoors and slammed the door. Peeping through the window, she could see him standing on her path, his face creased with annoyance, until he turned and went slowly away.

When she had time to think, Jane considered Arthur's words about Jethro. If it was true and he was to fight in Russia the chances of him returning to her were slim. What had happened to the plan to make a life for them all? Perhaps she should be sensible and take note. She was thirty and time was passing. The years went so quickly. Soon she would be approaching forty. Her attraction to Jethro, though profound and all consuming, could be seen as a foolish obsession grown out of loneliness and emotional deprivation. Her need for someone to hold, and to hold her, after years of grieving for Dan could well have distorted her judgement. And today she had seen a hint that Arthur could be affectionate. Men of his generation were generally unwilling to make themselves vulnerable to a woman by revealing their feelings. Arthur was no exception to this tendency. Was she being foolish, hanging on to a dream and refusing the one chance she would ever have to escape this arduous battle out of poverty? Wouldn't it be lovely to be able to wear a new dress and give the girls something that was newer even than fifth hand, something pretty that fitted them?

These thoughts occupied Jane on a Wednesday and it wasn't until the following Saturday that she was aware that Silas was again in the area. They were preparing to go to the Ward's Wood and she had packed a simple picnic. As they walked up the track in the direction of the farm, Jane felt Nancy pulling at her skirt.

'Ma, there's someone following us. He keeps hiding every time I look but I saw him.'

Jane looked around but could see nobody. 'You have a look, Beccy.'

'It's Mr Roberts, Ma. Why is he following us? Shall we just ignore him?'

'If he hasn't gone by the time we reach the farm, I'll fetch Mr Ward. He will send him off.' Jane walked a little faster, urging the girls to stay close.

When they reached the five-bar gate, Silas was no longer attempting to hide but ambled in full view a few yards behind them. They stood as Jane called, 'Arthur!' in as loud a voice as she could. Almost immediately he came out of the house. When he reached the gate, he and Jane exchanged a few words then she stood aside and turned to face Silas who came closer.

Arthur called over to him. 'So it's you again. What have you got to say this time?'

Silas had his hands in his pockets and the bowler sat at the back of his head. 'Took no notice, did you. Gotta make this clear. You got no business with this 'ere woman. She's my Dinah, not yours. I bin courtin' her for years. We got an understandin' goes way back and you's not wanted.' He turned to Jane. 'Tell him, Jane. Tell him you's bin mine from when you was a girl an' no one's marryin' you but me.'

Arthur was frowning as he turned to Jane. 'Is what he says true? Have you got an understanding?'

'No, I have not. He lives in a fantasy world. I keep telling him but he won't take no for an answer.'

Arthur unlatched the gate and came out on to the track. 'Then perhaps we should make things clear to him once and for all, in the time-honoured way if necessary. Then he'll get the message.' He walked up to Silas whom he expected to back away. However, Silas stood his ground.

'I's not afraid of the likes of you,' and he put up his fists, looking like a huffing and puffing overweight bullfrog. Jane could see Arthur was clenching and unclenching his fists too, eyeing his adversary with a practised eye. Then suddenly they were on each other,

260

struggling to find an opening where an effective punch could be laid. Arthur was the older of the two but Silas's dissolute ways had taken their toll. Apart from a lot of grunting and grasping as the two men grappled around one another, it was a pretty ineffective fight.

Nancy hopped up and down on the verge and giggled, Rebecca stood by with her hands over her mouth in alarm and Jane merely watched two elderly men fail to land any but the smallest of blows. Arthur managed to land one good one at last and socked Silas full on the nose, tipping him backwards into the dust. He was on his feet in an instant and backed away. Arthur stood flexing his arms and looking after him. 'You bugger off. If she's marrying anyone, she's marrying me.'

With a growl and much shaking of fists, Silas sloped away.

Soon all was quiet. 'I think that has sorted him,' Arthur said. 'I hope you don't mind my jumping the gun there, but I thought it the best way to get the message across.'

Jane laid a hand on his arm. 'Don't concern yourself, Arthur. Did he hurt you? I must thank you for defending me.'

'Hurt me? Of course not,' he said, gingerly rubbing his shoulder. 'Do you want to come into the house for a moment?'

But Jane declined. Her nerves were jangling and she needed to sit quietly to calm down. She wanted to sit among the trees or by the stream where she and Jethro had talked together. The fight was nothing, but it was time to assess how she felt about letting all the memories of Jethro slip into the past forever, untainted by any expectations or hopes for the future. They had to go. It was a new future that must preoccupy her now for it was more and more likely that the die was cast. She would have to marry Arthur. She would accustom herself to the idea and she would go through with it and do her best to embrace a new life as a farmer's wife.

There was some comfort in making up her mind, there, in the tall grass with the trees swishing gently overhead and the sound of the water trickling over the cold grey stones.

CHAPTER 23

Silas turned up once more at Jane's door. Her heart sank when she saw him. When would he accept defeat and leave her alone?

'What do you want NOW?' she cried.

This time, making a show of much sorrow, he berated her for setting a bully on him. 'I was jest wantin' to talk to you, to offer you the greatest treasure I own. Myself, lock, stock, and barrel.'

Jane sighed. 'Tell the truth, Silas, you were spying on us. And he was not bullying you.'

'What? He knocked me down. What's that if it ain't bullyin'? Nearly broke my nose, 'e did. Bin snortin' blood for days.'

'And were you not trying to do the same to him?'

'But Jane,' he wailed. 'What's happened to you and me? You's treatin' me very bad. What have I done to deserve such treatment from my best girl? I's done nuthin' but good to you.' It was true that Silas's nose was more bulbous than usual and sported blue, purple and yellow, which made Jane smirk a little.

'It served you right. If you don't leave me alone, he might do it again, so be warned.' Jane had had enough of this conversation and wanted him gone.

'So you won't be takin' me up on me offer?'

'What offer was that?'

'What I said, lock, stock and barrel.'

'Too late, Silas, the banns have been posted.' It was a flip, impatient remark, intended to finally send him away. It was a lie, but she reckoned he was unlikely to go to the church to check. Marry him? Did he never look at himself in a mirror? She never rated herself any more desirable than any other woman but surely he could see how impossible their match would be. Jessie would have suited him better. Jane turned from him and began to close the door but the sight of his reaction shocked her.

He gave a roar of rage, stamped his feet and a flush of crimson suffused his pock-marked face. His nostrils flared and a pulse beat in the veins of his forehead. He began shouting, kicking the step, throwing his arms wildly about.

'You bitch, you harlot, you led me on. Now you treat me like dirt. Well, if I can't 'ave you, no one will, I'll see to that. You think I'm shit, do you? Well, you'll pay for that.'

Jane took a step back, horrified at this response. She had experienced his tactics before but nothing as extreme as this. She put out a hand to calm the frenzy and say something to placate the raving individual before her but he spat on the ground at her feet.

'You'll not marry 'im. I'll make sure o' that. You gonna regret this, Jane Chapman, by God you will.'

Since there was nothing to be done, she slammed the door on him and bolting it, leaned against it, her heart pounding. He hammered on the other side; she could feel the blows through the wood. He kicked and punched for several minutes and then there was silence.

'Beccy, look out and see if he's gone.'

Rebecca ran to the window and peered out. 'He's in the lane, Ma, waving his fists at us.'

Jane relaxed a little. 'We all stay in here now until we are sure he's gone.'

An hour later, when everything in the lane was quiet in the fading light, Jane told the girls to bolt the door behind her and stay quiet until she returned. 'I'm just going to run up and see Arthur,' she told them.

She had thought over the encounter with Silas and was worried. He meant to harm her in order to stop the supposed marriage. He might even be determined enough to attack her, maybe even kill her, for he certainly had given every appearance of murderous intent. His words, *If I can't have you then no one will,* echoed time and time again in her mind. There was no telling what he might do and she did not feel safe.

At the farm, she hammered on the house door.

'Jane, Jane, what is the matter? Come inside.'

She grabbed his arm. 'Arthur, it is Silas Roberts, he has threatened me. He went wild and I'm afraid he'll do something violent to hurt me.'

'Sit, woman, and tell me calmly what he's done.'

There was reassurance in his calm manner and at once she felt he would protect her. He made her sit by the fire and listened as she told him of the clash at her door.

'I'm afraid he means to harm me but it's my fault because I told him we had called the banns.'

Arthur opened his eyes wide. 'Did you, now?'

'I know, I shouldn't have lied but I wanted him gone for good. But I was only voicing what I had decided because I will marry you, Arthur, if you still want me.'

He looked hard at her. 'Are you sure, after all this time?'

'Yes.' Jane said only this one word, not wanting to express the reasoning that had obsessed her up until that moment of decision, the weariness and the fear. Finally after waiting over a year without a word, the time had come to forget any hopes or expectations of a different outcome. She was hoping he would not mention Jethro, would not want her to tell him she no longer thought of him. It would hurt too much to have to say the words. Fortunately, Arthur said nothing but got up and went to the dresser and from a drawer, took a small box.

'Wear this for me, Jane, to cement your promise. It was my mother's ring. My wife wore it until she died and now I'm giving it to you. And I think we must marry as soon as possible, then Roberts will not dare to do anything to you or he will have me to deal with.'

Jane took her time down the track home. It was decided and she should have felt relieved but instead a small germ of doubt plagued her. No matter how many times she listed the benefits of marriage to Arthur, questions arose in her mind. Had she made the right decision? Would there be regrets later? There was no going back now so it would be up to her to make the move the right one. And if there were to be regrets, well, she would just have to deal with them. She would do her best to make the marriage work. She would be practical and learn to live without passion, without love. Respect and some affection was all she had to give Arthur. But what of her girls, would they be glad? She would soon know because they would have to be told at once that their life was about to change.

As soon as she got in, she sat them down, saying, 'Girls, I have something to tell you. I have just agreed to marry Arthur in three weeks' time.' She paused, looking at the two young faces as the information sank in. Then Nancy grinned and clapped her hands.

'I am pleased, Ma. It means we can live on the farm, doesn't it? It's lovely up there and we shall have lots of animals to care for, and lots of room and nice food. When can we go?'

'Not till after the wedding, Nancy, but I am glad you are happy. What about you, Beccy?'

Rebecca was pensive. 'Are you glad, Ma, really?'

'Of course, dear,' Jane said firmly. 'He is a fine man and he will look after us. He has promised to send you both to school. That will be good, won't it.'

'But…'

'But what, Beccy?'

'But what about Jethro? I thought…'

'Yes, well, I have given up waiting for Jethro. I have come to the view that he has gone forever, so this is what I have chosen for all of us.'

'But what if he does come back?'

Jane's heart lurched at her daughter's words but she steeled herself to reply. 'I can't wait forever. We must move on. Be happy for me, Beccy.'

Rebecca smiled. 'If you are happy, Ma, then I am happy too.'

The real banns were called and posted on the church door the next day.

The next three weeks were hectic for there were decisions and arrangements to make. Now the whole village knew there was to be a wedding. There would be a feast after the ceremony at the farm and a cake had to be ordered. The gig had to be cleaned and polished and decked with ribbons and flowers on the day, for Jane and the girls would travel in it to the church. Arthur planned to arrive on horseback. All the village prepared to be there on the big day, for a wedding was an occasion for everyone to enjoy.

Though the work of the farm had to go on, efforts were made to keep the farmyard free of mess for once.

There was little for Jane to do but she was anxious about what she would wear. She sewed a new nightgown and a camisole and chemise and several petticoats but her boots were a disgrace, as were the children's. Finally she had to mention it to Arthur during one of their meetings.

'Of course you must have new boots and the girls too. And do you have a suitable gown?'

'But I don't need a new gown.' If the farm was not doing well, Jane didn't want to give Arthur this extra expense when Silvie had offered to lend her a gown when she heard the news.

'Are you sure? I could stretch to a modest gown,' Arthur said.

'It is only for one day, Arthur. I can organise a suitable garment for one day.' The truth of the matter was that Jane did not feel excited enough to make a fuss over the clothes she wore. Silvie's lavender dress which she had worn to her own wedding would do well enough.

It took a whole day to travel the eighteen miles to Bedford to buy new boots and then back in the afternoon. It was exciting for the girls to go to a city but Jane was apprehensive. It was many years since she had been in any but the meanest of shops or bought anything for any of them that was not worn many times by others, usually requiring mending, washing or altering to make them fit and all at as little cost as she could manage.

'For best effect you must have these. They are the height of good taste these days.' The sales woman took down a pair of white boots with scalloped edges and fancy patterns in blue and pink on the high heels.

Jane viewed them with a jaundiced eye. She wanted something she could wear every day and could not see herself stomping around the muddy farmyard in these.

How could anyone work in them? She would look ridiculous.

Finally she chose stockings and gloves and low slippers with a rosette on the instep and reckoned that would do for the wedding. 'I'll have a pair of serviceable everyday boots too,' she told the saleswoman, 'and something similar for the children.'

In the large emporium further down the road, where silk and grosgrain dresses in a multitude of colours and styles were on display, Jane allowed the girls to choose what colour they liked. Nancy chose pink with white pantelettes to hide the scarring on her leg. Rebecca chose blue and white stripes. The sales woman tried hard to sell Jane a crinoline which she said was very *à la mode* but had to be satisfied when Jane decided on only a tiered petticoat.

Arthur completed the trip by taking them to a pie shop for supper. They sat on a bench in a park afterwards to eat ices, the first the girls had ever tasted. Jane watched a cheerful Arthur tease the girls and laugh with them. Smiling as she watched, she told herself that perhaps life with him might not be too bad after all. Could she even learn to love him?

She decided in that moment to draw a mental ring around all she remembered of Jethro and save it as a beautiful memory. Why had she supposed Fate would deal her such happiness? She knew of only a few who were so lucky and most were not. They struggled through as best they could and she must do the same. If Arthur gave her all he promised, she would indeed be fortunate but if not, she would make sure it was not her fault. Like everyone else she was forced to take what opportunities life presented and it would be foolish to reject them and if she had to harden her heart to get through, then so be it.

Jane gave a great sigh and sat back, watching the girls laughing. No matter how committed she was to what lay ahead, her heart would never be hard enough to resist the sudden memories that often swamped her with sadness. Some little thing, some swift reminder of what she had lost caught her when she least expected it. Sometimes it was Stevie, sometimes Jethro, sometimes

Dan. A little snatch of music which had meaning, the sight of may blossom in the lane or a full moon in the garden all disarmed her. These moments ambushed her and she wondered how long she would have to endure them. Or maybe they were precious to be garnered like gems to lighten lacklustre days.

Soon they climbed aboard the gig and made for home, crushed together, where Nancy fell asleep. It was the girls' first visit to a city and the day had been a thrill for them.

CHAPTER 24

A week later the new clothes were delivered, to the girls' great delight. In the meantime they had made three circlets for their hair. As a widow, Jane was not expected to wear a veil for the wedding but with twisted stems laced with wax flowers and ribbons, their handiwork made a charming final touch.

On the day, Jane put on her new chemise and the stiff petticoats and the white stockings secured with a pair of their home-made garters. Then she put on Silvie's lavender skirt, arranging all the generous fabric over the undergarments. Next, she put on the bodice and buttoned it from neck to the pointed waist, and then her slippers and the circlet on her dark hair that had been tamed for the occasion. She stood in front of her daughters who looked in awe at their transformed mother. 'If only Jethro could see you,' trilled Nancy. Jane had to spin round to hide the lump in her throat and the tears that threatened to spill down her cheeks. 'Don't say that,' she blurted out. Rebecca took Nancy's arm and touched her lips with a finger.

Soon the girls were enjoying their outfits too. They twirled and pranced about the room, admiring each other but then, in a quiet moment Rebecca asked Jane, 'Are you happy, Ma?'

Jane turned to her sensitive little daughter who always seemed to be tuned to Jane's feelings and now had perhaps sensed the tumult inside her mother.

'Of course,' she replied, smiling. Then why did it feel as if she was walking into the lion's mouth? She had made her decision and a greater part of that had been to give the girls a better life. There was no regretting that. Admittedly fear had struck her when Arthur's patience was about to give out but a Workhouse future had been avoided and security lay ahead. She had seen the best of Arthur: his generosity and his steadfastness, and she had seen some of the worst: his sharp temper and his uncompromising hardness, and she hoped to be able to cope with those. So there should be no reluctance on her part and certainly not the deep grumbling sense that this was all a bad mistake.

'Yes, Beccy, I am happy and I hope you are too.' What else could she say? At that moment the cart pulled up at their door.

Tom was driving and the girls rushed out into the sunshine to admire the horse who had ribbons plaited into her tail and a garland of flowers around her neck. They climbed aboard and Jane sat between them and they set off along the lanes to the village. Some villagers were at their doors, waving and wishing Jane well as they passed. As they approached the church they saw a gaggle of villagers all waiting by the door. The vicar was waiting there too beside a couple who came forward as soon as the cart pulled up.

This was the cousin from Dunstable, Jane surmised, as he handed her down.

'Thomas Ward, and this is my wife Edith. I am pleased to meet you at last, Jane, and happy to welcome you into the family.'

The woman grasped Jane's hand. 'Oh yes, so pleased. Such a happy outcome for Arthur.' She was dressed in the latest fashion with flounces and frills in striped silk in yellow and green with a bonnet to match. Then she turned to Nancy and Rebecca and made a fuss of them, declaring what pretty things they were.

Jane was unsure what to make of Thomas. In appearance he was older and more substantial in his build than Jethro and had the air of a successful business man, as she knew he was. His wife chatted volubly but Thomas had a restraint about him. He watched Jane with a sombre expression while his wife flitted gaily about. Jane wondered what thoughts were going through that self-contained head and it occurred to her that later, if she got the chance, she might discover from him what had happened to Jethro, for he would surely know.

The vicar came down the path to the group. 'Shall we go into the church?'

They all grouped themselves into a line but at that moment, Arthur rode up. He was wearing a top hat, a smart coat and a silk neckerchief in bright yellow. The crowd parted to let him through and Tom took hold of the horse's bridle.

Arthur smiled down at Jane and stood in the stirrups, preparing to slide his leg over the horse to the ground. As he stood, well above the heads of the crowd with his back towards them for an instant, a shot rang out, and then a second. There were surprised cries from the villagers as Arthur slumped forward over the horse's back but then the crowd fell silent.

All the group were turned back to welcome Arthur, they gaped and were still, shocked at what they saw. The horse moved restlessly, held tightly by Tom, who gaped in horror at his boss. Then Arthur fell backwards to the path and lay still on his back. Women in the crowd screamed. Jane rushed to the prone body and dropped to her knees. 'Arthur, Arthur!' she cried, touching his face with both hands. She crouched over him while behind her Thomas stood looking down at his uncle.

There was a shout from the crowd and everyone turned to face the speaker. It was Silas Roberts holding a rifle. His face was scarlet 'I told yer, didn' I. I warned

281

yer. He'll not 'ave yer.' He hurled the rifle to the ground, turned his back and walked away but not before Jane glimpsed an expression of triumph on his face. Nobody moved to stop him.

Thomas took hold of Jane's arm to pull her upright but she shook him off and turned again to Arthur. 'Move out of the way, Jane,' he instructed, so then she did as she was told, standing close as he turned Arthur over. Two bullet holes in his back seeped blood onto the path. Thomas felt for a pulse in his neck then shook his head. No need to say that his uncle was dead.

Jane burst into tears. The two girls and Edith stood a little way off, horrified and speechless. The vicar joined Thomas, looked down, then took Jane by the arm and led her away to the church porch where he sat her down on the concrete seat there. Edith and the girls joined her. By now Nancy was crying. Edith was clasping and unclasping her gloved hands, her face distraught. 'What a terrible, terrible thing. Who is that man?'

Jane was unable to respond. The shock had deprived her of speech, even thought, and she just sat, as white as a statue, devoid of feeling.

She wasn't aware of what happened next but learned later that Edith took charge of the girls and took them to the farm. Jane had spent some time in a pew in the empty church while the crowds outside dispersed. Arthur was lifted on to a back pew and the constables were sent for. A long time afterwards, Jane found herself back in her own cottage with Silvie, who stayed until Jane's senses revived and she begged to be left alone.

Another death, another sorrow. What had she done to deserve yet another loss – Dan, Stevie, Jethro, who was as good as dead to her, and now Arthur? Was it God or the Fates who decreed that she must lose all those she loved best?

She took off the dress, tore the circlet from her hair and put on the black garment she had worn for Dan and Stevie. Was it best that the marriage had not taken place? She could not decide. She just felt that Arthur had been a good man and she would have learned to love

283

him in time. Now it was back again to the beginning, she thought sardonically, back to poverty, to unrelenting work after a near miss at something better. With that thought she reproached herself. It was Arthur who was dead and that was what really grieved her because she had thought unkindly of him when he had proved himself generous and kind to her.

Jane sat in her old black dress before the dead fire, reliving the afternoon and agonising over Silas Roberts. Everyone in the village knew him and stood looking elsewhere as he fired the gun. What they made of his words, she could not imagine but she wondered how she could have been so stupid as to suppose he intended to harm her. Of course he had Arthur in mind. He wanted to remove his rival and make the way clear for himself, except that now he had only succeeded in making his way clear to the gallows.

Her mind was full of regret and sorrow. She rocked back and forth in the chair, her arms clasped about her middle until, hearing a knock on the door, she opened it to find Thomas frowning as he inspected the front of the cottage. 'Oh good, I have the right place. Can I talk to you, Jane?'

Wordlessly she let him in. He stood still for a moment looking round, surprised, she thought, to find such a rough interior, the clothes left on chairs, the worn furnishings, the obvious poverty. It occurred to her that, seeing her at the church in such finery had misled him. Surely Arthur had told him she was poor but he had not appreciated quite what that meant in the rural villages.

Collecting himself, he turned to her. 'Edith says she will have your girls for the night if you agree. She thinks you may need some time to yourself.'

Jane nodded and pulled a chair for him to sit. 'She is very kind. That would be best.'

He cast an eye over the chair before he sat. 'How are you? We are both devastated by this terrible turn of events and wonder what you will do now.'

'It is kind of you to concern yourself with me. Life will go on for me as before. We were not married so I have no claim on your family.'

'Oh, that would never do. We shall always consider you as part of our family. You were so close to Arthur and would have made him happy, but tell me, who was that man who shot my uncle?'

Jane told him briefly about Silas, about how he had fantasied for a long time about courting her and finally allowed jealousy and spite to distort his mind. 'He threatened to stop the wedding, you heard him, but I never imagined this.'

'Well, he's been caught and arrested, I hear, so he won't cause any more trouble for you and I hope he hangs for the killing.' He said these last words with a vehemence that made her look up.

'But where did he get the gun?' Jane said, 'I am sure farmers around here only have shotguns for game and rabbits, not for people.'

'I am told a friend lent it to him. The landlord of a public house in Flitwick. His son is due to join his regiment on the ship off to the Crimea. We are fighting a war there, you know.'

'I heard of it,' she replied.

'Yes, the young soldier was persuaded to lend the rifle to this Silas. The police have it now so the young man is going to be in trouble for the loss of his weapon.'

'Arthur told me Jethro had gone to Russia to fight for England.'

Thomas looked briefly at her then turned away. 'Oh, did he say it was definite?'

'Do you think it was true?'

Thomas leaned forward, clasping his hands between his open legs, his head low. 'I can't tell you that.'

'Because you don't know, you mean?'

Thomas nodded.

'But he told me Jethro went to you when he left the farm.'

'Yes, he did come, angry, confused, his head full of wild ideas, many of them about you.' He looked up at her and smiled then averted his gaze once more.

'About me? What sort of ideas?' She could not resist asking.

'Oh, I can't remember. It is over a year ago.'

Yes, a painful, desolate year, thought Jane. 'So he may have gone for a soldier?'

Thomas shook his head. 'He never told me one way or the other.'

She looked thoughtfully at him, thinking it was unlikely that the two men had not sat for at least one evening talking possibilities, exchanging views and advice about openings and coming to some sort of decision, but clearly Thomas was discomfited and evasive. He seemed determined to tell her nothing. However, it was callous of her to persist in enquiries about Jethro when Arthur was lying dead. 'Where have they taken Arthur?' she asked.

'He's at the farm. We thought it best to keep him close until the funeral. I shall have that to arrange. You will be there, of course.'

Jane frowned. 'Should I? I am not family now.'

'No, but close enough. Of course you must be there. You will lead the mourners in procession.'

Jane looked down and indicated her worn black dress. 'Like this? I will disgrace you all.' A lavender dress would not do at a funeral.

He stood. 'We will be glad to help you in any way we can. We shall always think of you and the girls as part of our family, in an informal way since the marriage never took place, but no matter.'

Jane murmured, 'You are very kind.' She would be glad to have people resembling relations in the area, even informal ones, but she suspected the connection would be short lived. Soon things would be back as they had always been, but without Arthur, Stevie and Jethro. That would be her bleak future, she was sure. She led him to the door. He took one last look around the room as she said, 'Say goodnight to Rebecca and Nancy for me. I will come for them tomorrow when I come to see Arthur.'

'There is much to do. We have decided to make a trip home to Dunstable but will be back in the afternoon. We'd like to take the girls too.'

Jane nodded her agreement and gave him a wan smile. She was weary and would no doubt sleep late in the morning.

CHAPTER 25

The next afternoon, Jane walked up the track to the farm carrying a bag of the girls' old clothes. There was a wreath of laurel hanging on the farmhouse door and all the curtains and blinds were tightly closed. Inside, she found all the mirrors draped with black crepe and the door knobs swathed in black too. Pictures had been turned to the wall and photographs laid flat. Edith had wasted no time.

The house was hushed. Rebecca and Nancy came to meet her, looking subdued and talking in quiet voices.

'Girls, I've brought your usual clothes. You must change at once.'

'Do we have to send our new dresses back, Ma?' Nancy asked.

'No, dear, they are yours to keep but they will not do for the mourning. Here, Rebecca, take them. Where is Arthur lying?'

'He's upstairs. We've been up to see him,' Rebecca replied.

Jane shooed them back into the downstairs room, saying, 'Wait for me. I'll see you later.'

She found Arthur in one of the empty bedrooms with Edith in a chair by him. He would be watched every moment he was in the house and she appeared pleased to have Jane replace her. Arthur lay still and cold in an elaborate casket surrounded by a profusion of flowers and wreaths.

As she left, Edith whispered, 'Thomas has arranged it all, the undertaker, the hearse, everything. Now he's gone to see about the printing of memorial cards and a photographer too because we must have cards to send. You will want a memento of Arthur, won't you?'

'Of course.' Arthur was still wearing his wedding suit. Jane hoped there would be no need to move him into a sitting position beside his living relatives as was sometimes done. Lying asleep among the flowers would be better. When Edith had gone, she gazed into his pale face, imagining some small movement of lip or eyelid to indicate that life had returned, but of course there was none. As the hours went by, Jane's mind roved in the silence over the ordeal of the coming funeral and what lay in store after that. Then Edith called her down for some lunch and they spent a quiet half hour at the kitchen table.

As Jane prepared to return to the 'wake', Edith said, 'I have a mind to lend you clothes for the funeral, Jane, in four days' time. I have spare black gloves and a veil, and a black dress you can borrow. I take it that skirt you have on was once black; the dye has faded, I can see. You know you will be the centre of attention to those who know your story.'

'If you wish.' Jane did not care, for it was only for a day, after all. Her old dress would do for the months following. Being poor, she would not be obliged to follow the conventions that wealthier people held to. She had changed from black to grey quite soon after Stevie's death for the death of a child was barely considered by some folk. Arthur was not her husband so in a few months a sombre grey would do, without her appearing insensitive.

The black dress Edith lent her was black silk with pearl buttons and tiny frills part way down the skirt. Jane considered it just about acceptable but had it been more elaborate she had been prepared to refuse it. She covered her face with the veil and steeled herself for the ceremony. At the farm gate the wagon waited to lead them in procession. It was a black four wheeled wagon, not elaborate with decorated glass and brass fittings, for Arthur was not rich enough for such extravagance. But the horse was black and a black clad undertaker took his seat to drive down to the church.

They proceeded down the track in silence. Jane compared this procession with Stevie's funeral not so long before. He had been wheeled to the church in a hand-wheeled bier, the tiny coffin jerking and bouncing over the stony parts of the lane, and it made her sadder to remember it. But she could not weep for Arthur now, though it would have been appropriate. She had cried enough and relied on the veil to disguise her dry eyes.

The interment was a sorry business. The vicar made the most of the moment as the coffin sank into the ground. Each mourner threw in a handful of dust and it was that moment that affected Jane the most. So sorry, Arthur, she repeated over and over to herself for she believed she had not behaved well.

Back at the farm, a variety of food and drink had been laid out. Jane stood with her back to a wall and watched the mourners throw off their sadness. Glad that the glum business of the day was over, they chatted, ate and drank. She was an outsider in this gathering and was eager to get away. Her daughters were eating their fill, giggling as they tasted and compared the unfamiliar food, and Edith was circulating among the dark suits.

Over on the other side of the room, Thomas took out his pocket watch and frowned as he registered the time, then replaced it in his waistcoat. Was he eager to have this all over too? He glanced around the room, searching, caught her eye and smiled, turning at once to talk to a woman standing near. Jane watched him check his watch three more times before she felt able to leave.

When she went to say her goodbyes, Edith said, 'Keep the dress, Jane, you look so well in it. I can get another if, God forbid, I should need one.' She put a friendly hand on Jane's arm. 'I am sure we shall be seeing you very soon,' and the two women parted as friends.

Glad to be alone at last but preoccupied with her thoughts Jane walked down the track. Nearing the lane she saw Jessie standing at the end of the path to her cottage. Turning as Jane approached, the woman waited, hands on her hips until Jane was closer.

'So, you're not goin' to be rich after all. Now there's a turn up. Just shows how the best laid plans, eh? Thought you was goin' to hoodwink that poor old man into marryin' you, didn't you. Serves you right, Miss High and Mighty. And here's me thinkin' I could move into your cottage when you'd gone. Ah well, as I say, best laid plans.'

Jane stopped, a yard or two off and listened to this poisonous tirade thinking it was no less than she expected from Jessie. She walked on, pushing past the woman to go to her door.

Ignored, Jessie found a second wind. 'And that poor old Silas Roberts, you treated him something shockin' and now that's the end of him. That's your doin'. And then there's that Jethro. Lucky escape for him, I say. Havin' a wild old time, I shouldn't wonder, sowin' his wild oats as is right and proper, 'stead of saddlin' himself with a couple of kids and Miss Fancy Pants.'

'Go away, Jessie,' Jane cried, hiding the tears that sprang to her eyes, and she hurried to close her door on the woman. She stood leaning against the wood, the tears streaming down her cheeks. Was that to be the estimation of others in the village? Did people think her proud and undeserving? Most hurtful of all, was there truth in what Jessie said about Jethro? The thought robbed her of strength and she sank to the floor and wept, for herself, for Arthur and all the empty future opening before her.

Rebecca and Nancy came home later and, matching their mood to their mother's, spent a quiet few hours before bedtime. When they were safely in bed, Jane walked around the cottage into the vegetable garden. She was in a strange mood, tired yet restless with a sense of anticlimax and disappointment. The encroaching dusk was calming. A mist was gathering and beginning to swirl around her, hinting at the autumn to come. She needed to be alone to think, to readjust to some kind of new beginning, or more rightly, the reestablishment of something old. She was heartsore and the coming night tuned exactly with how she felt.

CHAPTER 26

She stood in the middle of their remaining crops. Some remained to be picked… the cabbages, those not ravaged by the caterpillars, and there were beets and turnips left for later – all that Jethro had sown and she had cultivated over the months. Standing on the tilled soil with a hoe in her hand, she listened to the sounds of the night.

You have kept it well. It was a voice in her head. Her imagination was playing tricks but it was just like Jethro's voice, so familiar that it brought a tremble all through her. It seemed so real that a thrill shot from the pit of her stomach to the roots of her hair. Lifting her head she gazed ahead, seeing a vague shape on the path through the mist. Was it a ghost, or his spirit, come at last to comfort her? The spirit figure moved, came closer and became more defined. Was this the dead Jethro come to seek her out before he was gone forever? She peered into the filmy cloud as the figure took shape before her, then a dizziness swelled over her and she fell to her knees in the dirt, the black folds of the borrowed dress ballooning around her. 'Are you his spirit?' she gasped.

'No, real flesh and blood, my darling.' The figure came closer and she saw it was him. Hardly believing her eyes she held out her hands and felt the hard, calloused skin of his real hand grasp her own.

He pulled her up and enclosed her in his arms, supporting her, for all the strength had gone from her limbs. 'Jethro, my love, you've come back to me,' she murmured weakly.

'I said I would. How could you doubt me?'

'But so long. I've waited so long.'

'There were reasons. Let's go inside and I will tell you everything.'

They clung to each other and went indoors. In the light of the candles, Jethro looked at her in the silk dress, with the pearl buttons twinkling and her same eyes, holding his as lovingly as before. 'You are just as beautiful as I remember,' he said.

'And you, Jethro, are stronger and bigger than I remember. Do you still feel as you did before, only I thought perhaps...'

He strode swiftly to her, took her face between his two hands and looked earnestly into her eyes. 'Never doubt it for one moment.' His hands slid down her body, remembering the softness, the curves, and then with a desperate eagerness, he began to pull the bodice from her shoulders, sinking his face into the crook of her neck. She felt an answering urgency and began to tear at the shirt on his back. Stumbling backwards they fell together on to the daybed in a frenzy of entwined limbs, touching, stroking, kissing just as in the old days. They lay together with such gladness, murmuring together, renewing the old vows and merging one with the other in a delirium of lovemaking.

Damp and exhausted, they lay afterwards until their hearts ceased pounding, and then they talked. He said, 'I expected to be at my father's funeral but I was delayed.

Thomas knew I was coming but I told him not to tell you. When I heard of the wedding I could not in all justice come to prevent it. I thought you had forgotten me.'

'And I thought you were dead. Arthur told me you were over the sea fighting and would surely not survive. I delayed until I thought there was no hope.'

'Did you not remember what I said?'

'Oh yes, but times were bad and I was so very low, especially when I lost Stevie. There were times when we hardly had food on the table. And Arthur was kind.'

'Oh, my dearest, I didn't know things had got so bad. Did he put pressure on you?'

'Never, but sometimes impatient with me when time and time again I put him off until I had no other course.'

'And that plait dealer fellow, that Roberts, did he make trouble for you?'

'Often, but I put him off too.'

'Why was he so persistent? So determined to have you? Thomas told me what he said as he walked away.'

'It is a sorry tale. I never told Dan but I want to tell you. Silas Roberts was my mother's plait dealer and when she was dying, I looked after her. I had to deal with him then. I was sixteen, naive and stupidly impressionable. He was younger at that time and not the wreck he is now and I was seduced by his promises. He would take me for drives in his gig, but one day we had an accident and I was thrown to the road. He told me that he had picked me up and carried me to my own front door. I was out cold for a bit so I don't remember but he claimed afterwards he'd saved my life and I owed him. But never mind all that now. Tell me, Jethro, where have you been all this time?'

'In the morning, dearest. I will tell you all then,' and turning, he groaned and reached for her again.

The sun was well up when Rebecca came rushing down the steps in her nightgown, standing open-mouthed when she saw the two bodies on the daybed. Her gasp woke her mother, who sat up, moving aside the male arm enclosing her. 'Look, Beccy, Jethro has come back. Pass me that shift, will you.'

Jane made herself decent and bustled about, tidying clothes strewn on the floor and making a fire to boil the kettle for morning tea. Jethro soon woke, stretched and yawned, and commented on how pretty Rebecca had become until she blushed and rushed back up the steps to wake Nancy and tell her the news.

Nancy smiled at Jethro when she came down but said nothing. However, in a quiet moment when the adults talked, she whispered to Rebecca. 'Does this mean we aren't going to live on the farm? I was looking forward to that.'

Rebecca shushed her sister but Nancy was thoughtful. 'Jethro will have the farm now, won't he, so maybe it will be all right after all.'

Rebecca frowned and moved to sit at the table. Jethro was telling her mother how he had spent the last year and she wanted to listen.

'I have worked hard, Jane, and it has changed me. I have done all I planned and made a place for myself in the world. I'll tell you, but first I must explain that I have come a great distance from Northamptonshire. That is why I was late. I went to my Da's grave then saw Thomas, but for only a few minutes. I had to find you.'

Jane clasped her hands. 'Northamptonshire, is it a long way? But what about the farm? Will you stay, Jethro, and take it over?' Her heart sank as he shook his head.

'I can't stay here, and I do not want to be a farmer. I have talked this over with Thomas and he will put in a manager. The farm is not doing well and my Da was behind the times. My links are all with Northampton now.'

'Why that place? What is for you there?'

He told her how, since farming was all he knew, he had decided to visit all the manufacturers of farming machinery he could find to learn about the new inventions that were becoming popular on the bigger farms. With less manpower available and larger farms, there was a drive for more efficiency, more labour-saving machines. It had meant borrowing money from

Thomas and travelling first to Leighton Buzzard, then to another company in Suffolk, then Lincoln and later Devizes.

'The travelling was hard but I went wherever I could find one. I saw new sowing machines, seed drills, new threshing machines, steel ploughs and reaping machines. If only Da had known of them or could afford to buy any, the work would not have been so hard.'

Jethro looked around at the listening faces. 'When I reckoned I knew enough, I thought to start selling small tools that even the small farms use, things like rakes, scythes and sickles in steel, and grass hooks, even threshing flails. In a short time I moved on to steel ploughs and small horse-drawn seed drills. I was able to give advice, make recommendations and I could see the business would grow. But I was on the road a lot, visiting customers, buying and selling. I was so busy sometimes I didn't sleep for days. This was why I did not send you word.' He gazed at Jane, hoping she would understand.

'So you will go back to Northamptonshire.' Jane's voice betrayed her worry. Where did she fit in all this enterprise?'

'I must, but I want you to come with me. You probably know more about farming than you realise and you could be a great help to me. Together we can build the business, you and I.'

Of course she would go with him, anywhere in the world if he wished. Her future in Lilley was bleak. 'Do you have somewhere we can live?'

'At present I have a store room and I sleep on a truckle bed and eat in the nearest inn, but I can afford to rent a cottage in one of the many small villages near the city if you are agreeable.' He looked around the room. 'Somewhere better than this, I hope. And we'll get the girls into school and they can forget about straw plaiting. I am sure you girls will love that.'

Jane smiled at him. It might be a dream but she would do it. Anything to be with him. 'We are not wed, Jethro, could we defy the conventions like that?'

'I will if you will,' he replied, 'and after the mourning for my Da is done, we shall marry.

EPILOGUE

Rebecca woke and stretched, luxuriating in the comfort of the soft mattress beneath her. For an instant she didn't know where she was even though two weeks had passed since she slept here for the first time. The ceiling was white over her head and there were white muslin curtains moving gently in the breeze from the open window. Lifting herself on to her elbows she looked over to the other bed in the room where Nancy still slept. No hay crackled under her weight, no dust drifted down from the thatch. She was in their new cottage, far from Lilley and the lane, from Jessie and her noisy family, from the wood, the stream and the farm.

They had moved to Northamptonshire, four miles from the town of Northampton, to a village called Great Houghton, although to her there was nothing great about it. It was like any village but neater, with newer cottages. The cottage they were now in was nice, with bigger rooms and more of them. Cherry Tree cottage in Cherry Tree Lane; that was a pretty name. They had packed up their things and Jethro had brought them here. He was like a new father now but she didn't mind even though she had loved her real one so much and missed him every day of her life.

The door opened and her mother came in. 'Oh, you are awake. Have you forgotten it's your birthday?'

Her mother was wearing a white apron over her new dark green skirt. 'Wake Nancy up and come downstairs. We have a surprise for you.'

Her mother was happier these days, ever since the time Jethro came back. The two of them were always busy and pleased they were selling a lot, because living in this village was more expensive than their old one. There was more rent to pay and other things that cost money, like wages for Jenny (imagine, they now had a maid) and stamps and new clothes. Rebecca felt a pang sometimes for the simplicity of their life in Lilley. She missed the woods and the stream, the lane and the fields all around. Her father's and Stevie's graves were too far away to visit. Jane said they would all soon acclimatise and she supposed that was true. She even missed the plaiting just a little and the sewing too. These days she didn't know what to do with all the hours in the day.

Her mother bustled about the room, picking up clothes and reaching to hug Rebecca as she used to do. Her mother's hair no longer fell about her shoulders but was neatly contained under a white cap. It made her look a little older.

'Tomorrow is your first day at school. You haven't forgotten?'

'No,' Rebecca replied. thinking that first there was a whole day to fill with no straw plaiting, no sewing pincushions. At eleven she was too old to play and there was no fire to light, no water to fetch because now they had Jenny who came early to do all those things. How would she spend the hours? Nancy would want to explore, perhaps go to the river to watch the boats floating by, taking goods to and from the town. There were hides for the leather and shoe factories, and sand

and gravel for building the proposed new Guildhall –
that's what Jethro had said.

On her chair at the breakfast table she found a large
box. 'Open it, Beccy, it's for your birthday. You've
always wanted one,' said her mother.

Inside was a small bonnet, in a style she knew was
called a Dunstable, in fine straw plait with a wide blue
ribbon to tie under her chin. Silk flowers in many
colours decorated the crown and inside the brim there
was pleated blue silk.

'We bought blue to match the dress Arthur bought
you.'

'And to match the colour of your eyes,' added Jethro,
sipping his coffee.

Rebecca lifted it out and put it on to try. It was so
beautiful she knew it would look wonderful. This was
the first new thing she had ever had. She ran to the
mirror, smiling at her reflection. 'Oh thank you! Can I
wear it tomorrow to school?'

'Perhaps keep it for best,' Jane suggested. 'You are not going to grow out of it just yet.'

Nancy pushed a package across the table to her. 'I bought you something too.' It was a book, a reading book but with pictures too, called *Jane Eyre*. Her mother must have helped Nancy choose it because her sister never had more than a few pence and would not know where to buy a book or which one to choose. It was lovely to receive better presents than a yard of ribbon or a hair pin that Nancy would have bought out of her plaiting earnings.

'Now girls, Jethro has a delivery to make and I shall be busy in the store for most of today so you must entertain yourselves as best you can. Jenny will leave you some lunch and we will all meet up for a birthday tea.'

Rebecca sat in the new Windsor chair and watched her mother carefully wiping the table, then turning to adjust the two plaster dogs on either side of the mantel shelf. She straightened the picture of a kitten on the wall then turned the little vase of violets round to face the sun streaming through the open window.

Rebecca's new bonnet was on her lap and she examined the brim. The plait was very fine, much finer than she would ever have been able to do. It must have cost a lot of money and Nancy wanted one too but she would have to wait.

The store was not a shop but the smaller half of the cottage where Jethro kept all the tools and implements he sold. Rebecca had been inside and seen the displays of knives, shovels, clod hammers and other tools on the walls. On the floor were the bigger machines, a spike tooth harrow, a manure spreader, even a small wagon, but she had no idea what some others were for.

'Can we help you, Ma?'

'No dear, it is all writing work, lists and bills that you won't understand.'

The business was now a priority. Jethro said it kept the wolf from the door. It was different work but work all the same. Northampton was a smarter town than Luton with fewer poor people. It was busier and noisier and she hardly knew her way around the wider streets with their fine houses and buildings. She had been only once to All Saints Church for the wedding but was glad their new home was in a village.

'Shall we go and see who our new neighbours are?' suggested Nancy. 'And I want to look at the huge house behind the big iron gates. The people who live there must be awfully rich.'

'Lots of rich people live around here, Nancy. Jethro told me. They make a lot of shoes. We used to do plaiting and hats but here they make shoes and boots.'

'Are there no farms then?'

'Oh, lots, 'cos they buy things they need from Jethro.'

'That's a good thing, isn't it?'

'I guess so, but when I grow up I'm going to be a teacher and teach little children to read, like Ma's father was.'

'I thought she said he went round checking schools.'

'Yes, he did, but later. He started as a teacher.'

'Did he? Is that what Ma said?'

'He ended up as a Commissioner for Education.'

'Oh well, when I grow up I'm going to be rich. I'll be a fine lady and marry a rich man. Then I won't have to work at all.'

Rebecca smiled at her sister. She had learned in all her eleven years that you could never predict the future. You might have plans but everything changed all the time, sometimes for good and sometimes not and you had to be prepared to cope with anything. You could never tell what was coming your way.

END

About The Author

Janet Hutcheon now lives on Guernsey.She was born in the Midlands and after an early career in photography, became a mother, a teacher and then a welfare, training and human resources manager in an engineering company.

She now spends her retirement writing novels.

Other works by her include:

Toxic Games

What the Trees Saw

Ilse and the Painters

Within a Gilded Frame

These and other works can be found on amazon.co.uk

Printed in Great Britain
by Amazon

22695812R00178